BY PURE

CHANCE

By

PAUL 'POPS' WESTLAKE

CONTENTS

After accidentally running into his first love from over twenty years ago, Martin Gregson develops serious doubts about his current life and it begins to clearly dawn upon him that the feelings that he had for her back then, no matter how deeply planted, were still very much inside of him, and not being able to ignore or deny these feelings, he soon has to decide whether he should risk ruining his marriage for a chance of reliving the past, for a chance of true happiness, or stay in something that's solid and not broken and live in contentment.

1

It was a cold winter's night. Not a stormy or snowy night, but just a cold and clear night where a half moon shone almost as brightly as a full one and with a crispness in the air that you could snap like a twig between your fingers if you so wished. In one particularly quiet, and at first glance, ordinary looking street, there was a solitary woman. Walking up and down with her heels clipping hard into the pavement, minding her own business wearing a long black, but cheaply imitated fur coat to keep her warm as she momentarily paused to stand under a streetlight

Probably in an attempt to help cure her boredom, as there was no sign of anyone. Even The Sailors Arms at the end of the street was hardly making a sound, she first lights up a cigarette before taking out her mobile just to see if there were any messages or missed calls as Martin Gregson now found himself totally, and utterly lost and confused as he drove slowly along trying his best to get his bearings. He knew where he wanted to go and that was to a supposedly nearby Tesco's Metro which he had heard about, hoping to buy teabags and a Victoria Sponge Cake for himself and his wife whilst they watched a romantic comedy which had been regularly advertised during the week on Film4.

"Bloody useless sat nav," he moans. "Bet, it's Chinese crap," he continues moaning whilst taking another look at the screen. Not making head or tail of it at all. "If I follow this any longer I'll probably end up in Peking," he moans again turning away with no real intention of looking at it again as from now on, he'd rather trust his own sense of direction.

So slowly, he takes the next right and ends up in the quiet and ordinary looking street and as he surveyed the area the first thing that comes to his mind was, "Great, no sign of a Tesco's down here either." Defeat is immediately conceded and now he realises that there is nothing else for it, but to swallow his male pride and ask for directions.

On seeing the headlights that were clearly coming her way, the woman suddenly perks up and replaces her cigarette with a *Tic Tac* from her handbag and makes her way to the kerb in eager anticipation and luckily for her, the picked the exact spot where Martin had now pulled up as he winds his window down. "Excuse me, sorry to bother you, but do you know whether or not there's a Tesco's Metro around here somewhere?

It wasn't so much the question itself that took the woman slightly by surprise, it was more the way it was innocently put to her. "A Tesco's?" she asks in reply.

"Yeah. Promised the wife I'd get some teabags and a Victoria Sponge for the film tonight. Which will be starting soon so I need to get a move on."

These words from Martin appeared like music to the woman's ears. As she longed for that special man to be sitting beside her with tea and cake, or coffee and biscuits, anything like that whilst watching their favourite movie together just like any other normal couple. But it was just a pipe dream for now and she had to set her mind back into reality as she throws open her coat as Martin could clearly see that she was 'A Lady in Red', but not the Chris De Burgh kind, as her low cut dress displayed a very impressive cleavage that far outshone her face which clearly showed that she'd had a really hard paper-round.

"Well, darling," she began. "I can't quite offer you a Victoria Sponge and a night in front of the telly. I haven't paid my licence fee you see. But I can definitely offer you a much better time than that, which normally I'd charge fifty quid for, but, seeing how you such a good looking guy, and plus it's bloody cold out here, I'll make it forty, how's that?" she asks with a wink whilst at the same time deliberately leaning into his open window making sure that he caught a real eyeful of the goods that were now on offer.

Martin just couldn't help but gawp of what looked like two overinflated balloons which her black lace bra that was edging out of the top part of her dress struggling to keep them under control as she ensured that there was nothing else for him to look at for now, whilst making him feel like a boy who just had his first encounter with the opposite sex. And just like an innocent adolescent would, he began to blush which the woman thought was adorable.

"Aww, bless you sweetheart. There's no need to blush and be all shy with me. Trust me, I'll be gentle with ya," the woman says smiling away whilst continually happy to flaunt the goods.

"Err, I'm sorry, don't doubt you're a nice lady and all that but I'd rather not thanks as I've definitely turned into the wrong street by accident here," Martin says obviously now realising that he was certainly in the wrong part of town.

"Are you sure handsome? Promise ya, you'll won't regret it," she says as her greyish/blue eyes were doing their utmost to entice him into her clutches and Martin resisted and resisted as, all of a sudden, they were both to receive an unexpected surprise.

"Right you, hop it, and leave this man alone!" a woman shouts climbing into the passenger seat and slamming the door before she turns to Martin. "And if you don't want to get done for kerb crawling, then I strongly suggest that you get this car going right now! Just seen some coppers drive past here!" she continues to shout before buckling up her seat belt.

"Oi you, I saw him first," the woman in red fiercely protested at the other woman who just replied.

"Tough!" before she turns back to Martin. "Well, what are waiting for, to get arrested? Get a move on!"

By now, Martin clearly had the 'Rabbit in the Headlights' expression written all over his face as he looked at the two women who were now trading insults without any idea what was going on around him before he looking behind him to see if his now passenger, was actually telling the truth about seeing a police car. There wasn't any visible right now, but that didn't mean she was telling lies about what she saw. But he thought it wise not to stay around to find out as he then speeds away leaving the woman in red stamping her heels in anger.

"Right, you've got a choice now. You can either go right now and start heading up into the main part of town where there's more than likely to be plenty of coppers around patrolling seeing how it's a Saturday night and the pubs will no doubt be busy despite the cold or, you can go left, into the more quiet backstreets," the passenger suggests. Martin's only thought for now was not to be seen so on approaching the upcoming junction, he indicated and then turned left. He slows his speed down as his passenger then shuffles to make herself more comfortable before turning to Martin.

"Well, hello there. How are ya, alright? Bit chilly out there tonight isn't it but still, your car is nice and warm, lovely," she says in a bright and cheerful tone. The headlights were still very much in Martin's eyes as he remained virtually clueless into how he actually ended up with this strange woman in his car.

"What?" he asks.

"I said hello, and what a cold night it is tonight, and how your car is lovely and warm," she begins before continuing, "and seeing how you chose correctly and turned left, that makes you a clever boy with good judgement I see. There's a quiet little spot just over a mile or so further on. We can pull in there and you can tell me what you're fancying to do tonight."

The second he heard this, the fear in his eyes was clear for all the world to see and without really knowing what to say for now, he just kept driving whilst, more often than he would normally do, checking his mirrors and for now, thankfully, still no sign of any police car anywhere.

"Are you sure that there was a police car back there?" he eventually manages to ask.

"Yeah, of course," she begins. "Do I look like the kind of woman who would tell lies about something like that?" She asked that question with a clear twinkle in her deep blue eyes. Was it the high heels, fishnet stockings, tight black leather mini skirt, figure hugging white T-shirt and Denim Jacket that caused Martin to think that maybe she knew exactly what she was talking about, but the combination of deep red lipstick, blue eye shadow, mascara, and the long and permed dark brown hair and an expression on her face which clearly suggested that he'll never know for certain if she was telling the truth or not, cast a shadow of doubt over his mind. Either way though, he knew that he couldn't have her in his car for much longer so, he pulls over the first chance he had, which just happened to be behind a Kwik Fit which was situated at the corner of an Industrial Estate.

"How did you know that this was the quiet spot I had I mind? Have you been here before?" She starts to tease. "Oh, I bet you have, and more than once I reckon. You're a naughty boy, aren't you eh, lovely," she couldn't help but begin to giggle like a naughty schoolgirl whilst playfully stroking his hair with her fingers. Martin on the other hand, clearly was not seeing anything funny about this at all as he reaches across her. "Whoa easy now tiger, we haven't agreed a price or anything yet," she says still giggling. But Martin only had opening the passenger door and unclipping her seat belt on his mind, which he did in record time.

"Look, I'm sure you're nice enough and all that, but I'm not interested, okay. So, would you kindly get out of my car and leave me alone." He says not even wishing to look at her anymore.

"You just can't dump me here all by myself," the woman protested.

"I'm sure that you're a woman who knows exactly how to take care of herself," Martin says still refusing to look at her.

"I might get mugged or something even worse," the woman kept on protesting.

"If anyone is going to do any mugging around here, it'll probably be you."

"Oi, bloody cheek!"

"Get out of my car!"

"No!"

"I said get out of my car or I'll…" they both stopped arguing as they were suddenly hit by a set of headlights on full beam which temporarily blinded them both. It took a few seconds for their vision to return but when it did, they were both taken by surprise by the sight of a police car parked directly in front of them with a male constable behind the steering wheel and his female colleague in the passenger seat and both were looking straight at them with their own suspicions about what was actually happening right now as the male constable winds down his window and leans his head out. "Is everything alright?"

"I thought you said that the police would be in and around the town by now?" Martin mumbles to the woman.

"Normally they are, but this site is well known to them, as me and a few others sometimes use it. So, they've probably just driven around here on the off chance of catching someone at it," she mumbles in reply.

"Did you hear what I said? Is everything alright" The male constable asks becoming a touch impatient.

"Right, if you don't want me to start crying rape at the top of my voice. I suggest that you think of a way out of this very quickly," she mumbles.

"Why me?" Martin asks.

"Just do it," she says leaving Martin very-little choice in the matter, so he thinks hard for a moment, as he then has a flash of inspiration.

"Yeah, good evening officer. We were just driving around, and my friend here began to feel sick. Told her not to eat too much of that Chicken Madras. So, I pulled over because I'm not having her throwing up over these leather seats, you know what I mean."

It was abundantly clear that Martin would never make a good liar, and it was a good thing that they weren't in any interrogation room, because he would soon cave in. But there was nothing else to suggest that there was anything wrong going on so, and a touch disappointedly of not catching them at it, the male constable puts his head back inside, and pulls away as Martin breathes a huge sigh of relief.

"Bloody hell, that was too close for comfort," he says as the woman began laughing which causes him to give her the death stare. "What was so funny about that? Well, what?"

"Oh, lighten up will ya. They've gone now, so you can relax a bit. But it still might be an idea to drive somewhere else. Just in case they do a loop and come around again," the woman suggests seemingly knowing exactly what she was talking about.

"What do you mean drive somewhere else? Are you out of your mind? There's no way that I'm driving you anywhere! I have a wife waiting at home for me and the very last thing that I need is someone like you," Martin tells her meaning every single word.

"Wife at home you say, and you're driving around this part of town. That's not good is it? So, what exactly is it then darling? Problems in the bedroom department? She's not giving you exactly what you need? Has the thrill gone out of your sex-life and you're down here looking for some extra excitement?

"How dare you!" Martin says looking somewhat disgusted just at the mere thought of doing anything like she was suggesting and betraying his wife. "I'll have you know that I'm very happily married and devoted to my wife alright, and the only reason that I found myself around here tonight was due to the fact that I had got lost.

"The truth is I was out looking for a Tesco's Metro which is supposed to be around here somewhere, to pick up some teabags and a Victoria

Sponge, so that I can sit down with my wife and watch a film that we've planning to do all week, alright! Now, for the last time of asking nicely, will you get out of my car so I can return home to her?"

"No." The woman calmly says and still with a smile.

"No? What do you mean no?" asks Martin not being able to hide his frustration which just made the woman smile even more, clearly enjoying teasing him as she refuses to budge a single inch. Martin isn't usually the kind of man that gives in to temper tantrums or general bouts of anger, but the thought now of being able to get back to his beloved wife, with or without what he went out for, was really now beginning to push him over the edge.

"Right, for the last time, I'm telling you now, get out of my car or I'll…"

"Do what? Huh? What exactly are you going to do, call the police on me? Well go on, away you go then call them. Because if they do decide to turn up, I'll just cry rape or something like that. What are you going to do then eh? Come on big man, let's hear it." The prominent smug grin across her face really riled, Martin to a point of anger that he had never experienced before. And he wasn't quite sure how to handle it so, all he could do for now was just yell at her again.

"Get out of my car!"

"Don't you recognise me, Martin?"

And like if he had been hit over his head with a baseball bat, Martin just looked utterly dumbstruck as he just stared at the woman without a single clue who she was. Or what she was even talking about.

"What do you mean, do I recognise you?" Why on earth would I know who you are?" he asks still reeling from the question.

The woman leans a touch closer towards as she cordially invites him. "Take another look."

Martin studied and scrutinised every single inch of her face but still without knowing who she was, which the woman could see quite clearly so, she decided on another tactic.

"Try and picture me about a stone lighter, and with dead straight but short blonde hair."

Again, Martin scrutinised and studied as carefully as he could, but still without having any knowledge to who she was. Not giving up at all, the woman had one more card to play.

"It must have been about what, maybe even twenty years ago now, that we were sat next to your mum when she was in hospital, sleeping peacefully, after she'd suffered that minor heart attack and we promised each other that if anything like that happened to either one of us, then we'd be there for each other, no matter what."

His mobile started to ring. The screen said it was Vanessa. They both looked at it, the woman sort of guessed that it was probably his wife calling, probably wondering where he was and had he picked up the teabags and cake as the film was about to start. Martin took just one look at his phone. He just let it go to voicemail. "Wendy, is that really you?"

"I'm guessing that was your wife calling, you should have answered it. She's probably worried and wondering where you are," Wendy says.

"It's okay. I'll just tell her I was driving or something. Wendy. I mean, what, what's going on?" Martin asks scarcely believing what he was seeing.

"Yes, Martin, it's me. Small world isn't it, eh? So, what's a nice guy like you doing in a place like this?" Wendy asks deciding that maintaining a sense of humour right now would be the best course of action to take whereas Martin, still couldn't believe what was happening.

"Hang on. This can't be right. Wendy, what the hell are you doing?" he asks.

"Working."

"Well yeah, I can see that. I mean, why are you

doing, well, doing this?" he asks still shaking his head in disbelief.

"What can I say, Martin? Because, Virgin already have a Chairman."

Maybe it was still the shock of it all, but no matter how much Wendy put on a smile, Martin wasn't finding this funny at all, as he looks once again at the one who was his first true love, and now was, even though it was clear to see, refusing to believe that she had come to this.

"Just can't believe it. The last I heard about you must have been what, about ten years ago. You had your own business didn't you? Little florist shop, wasn't it? What happened to that? And weren't you married? Or at the least engaged?"

"Right, one question at a time alright," she begins. "Firstly, yes, I did have my own little florists, nice little shop as well. Okay, it was nowhere near on the same scale as Interflora, but it suited me and at the end of the day, it was mine. Yes, I was married. David his name was. Nice bloke, we we're happy for the first couple of years, or so I thought. It wasn't just the fact that he cheated on me which, and I know you'll think I'm mad, but I think I could have coped with that after a little while, but it was his gambling that really done it. Lost everything because of that. Our home and my business, that's when I decided that it was better to divorce him than do time for murder, which I did consider believe me. Family disowned me because of him, and I ended up with no one to turn to and rent and other bills had to be paid. So, here I am. Anyway, that's enough of boring old me, how about you? Married now I see. I'm not surprised about that, you always were the marrying kind. You had that matrimonial look in your eye."

"Matrimonial look?" he asks puzzled.

"Yeah. The settling down type. Safe. Dependable. A good and decent man," Wendy says with an honest smile which Martin did kind of appreciated.

"Thanks, that's nice of you to say so I suppose. But I was rather hoping for a more rugged, tough, manly bad-boy type of an image. Like that gangster programme of the telly what's it called again? Oh yeah, *Peaky Blinders*," Martin says rather more in hope than expectation which Wendy was very quick to confirm.

"No, Martin, you'll never be a gangster or any sort of bad-boy. It won't suit you at all. You just stay being the strong and reliable man that you are okay. Trust me, there's nothing wrong with that."

"Reliable?" he asks.

"Yeah."

"Strong?"

"Yeah."

"Oh really. What about good-looking or handsome then?" Martin asks albeit, a tad tongue-in-cheek but there was nothing at all funny about Wendy's answer.

"Of course, you're good-looking, you always were." And with that her blue eyes, came into direct contact with his green as they gazed and gazed without a single word being spoken, none were needed as undoubtedly Martin could clearly see that she had kept her looks. No doubt happy and fond memories came flooding back to both of them and the bond that initially brought them together in the past, was clearly still there, and as strong as it ever was. So strong in fact that Martin, whether willingly or not, leaned in for a kiss which brought Wendy suddenly back to life and turned away.

"So, have you been married long then?" she quickly asks while Martin now begins to feel a touch embarrassed by what he just tried to do.

"Seven years now."

"Oh, seven years is it," she begins. "Got an itch that needs scratching, have you?" She asks somewhat jokingly but that still couldn't hide any of Martin's embarrassment.

"Oh my God, I'm so sorry, what the hell was I

thinking of," he says as Wendy couldn't help but giggle.

"It's okay Martin honestly it is okay. So, calm down. It's nice to know that I've still got it," she then says.

"Got it? Of course, you've still got it. You'll never lose whatever it is. But honestly, I wasn't looking for any sort of itch to be scratch. I promise you that I wasn't and even if I was, I wouldn't be looking just to use you like that. And that's the truth."

"Getting the feeling, that somewhere amongst what you've just said, is a compliment tucked away somewhere," she says to which Martin only had one answer.

"Yes, there is. And it's a big one," he says to which Wendy graciously accepts before she says.

"Anyway, you say that you were shocked before, I couldn't believe my eyes when I saw you park up in that street earlier. And I knew that I had to rescue you from that Tanya.

"Oh, Tanya, was that her name was it? Not that I asked or was interested in finding out you understand. She even offered to knock ten pound off for me," he tells her.

"Yeah, I bet she did, the nasty cow. That's how she gets them you see. Flashing that fake chest of hers and offering discounts and when she's done the deed her pimp has a habit of showing up out of nowhere and mugging the poor punter for more money."

"Really?"

"Yeah, really."

"So, it looks like you came to my rescue. Thank you, but I have to say that you're the strangest looking Sir Galahad I've ever seen," he says with a smile.

"You're welcome and being honest you're the weirdest looking Guinevere that I've ever come across," she says sharing this little joke between them.

"Well, we always did say that we'd look out for each other, no matter what," Wendy then reminded him as Martin just nodded in acknowledgement as he remembered that very moment fondly.

"How could I ever forget," he begins before asking Wendy a question that, due to the moment they were now sharing, she clearly was not expecting. "Why did you leave me?"

Wendy instantly turned away from him. She had to. As she suddenly recollected how much she knew Martin must have been hurt by what she did. Even when she did find enough courage to answer him, for now, she still couldn't look at him.

"I know that I should have had the guts to tell you

to your face and not just send you a letter, and yes, I get, that I hurt you badly Martin, but believe me that was the very last thing that I ever wanted or even thought that I would ever do. But it's just like I said a few moments ago. You're the reliable, strong, dependable type of man. You were ready to settle down even back then. And I realised one day that quite simply, I wasn't.

"There were things that I wanted to do places that I needed to see long before I even thought about finally settling down. Things like going skydiving and travelling to places like Paris, Rome, New York, Hollywood amongst many others that I wanted to see at the time. I knew that if I'd stayed with you, then I would have never had done any of these things and in the end, I would have ended up hating you. And trust me Martin, I never wanted to end up doing that. You're just too good a person."

It was when she had finished speaking, that she eventually found the courage to look back at him as suddenly he then turns away trying to take in what he had just heard before eventually asking. "And did you?"

"Did I what?"

"Do all the things that you wanted to do and see all the places that you wanted to see?"

"Well, I did do the skydive many years ago for charity. It was amazing, honestly, what a buzz I got from it. Don't think I'll ever do it again mind, I think once was clearly enough for me. And I did manage to travel to most places I wanted to go. Apart from Hollywood. But hey ho, maybe one day."

By now, Martin was able to face her again and no matter how much she smiled, in a reassuring sense at him, he knew that deep down, she was putting on a brave face. And that, was hurting him badly.

"Wendy, look, how did you... I mean, what on earth happened to you? I just can't believe that you've been reduced to this."

"Hey Martin, it's okay. Like I said to you, I had no one to turn to, and I needed the money, and I needed it quick. I won't deny that the first time I did it, not only did I feel but I was physically sick, and the next couple of times after I felt so dirty that I would be in the shower for well over an hour at a time afterwards. But after a while, I just began thinking to myself that it's just turning a trick. And it means absolutely nothing. I just do it, smile, and take their money. Nothing at all emotional about it. Which means no one gets hurt and that's the way it should be. Just business. Nothing more, nothing less."

Maybe she was right, that it was just business and

nothing else and somehow, she'd become sort of immune to it. But that still didn't mean that Martin had to like it. Which he clearly didn't. "No, this ain't right," he says.

"What isn't right?" she asks.

"That you should be doing this."

"Doing what?"

"You know what. Selling yourself like this. It just isn't right," he says as Wendy, seeing how pained Martin was now in because of how he felt about her plight, attempted once again, to put a brave face on and make light of it.

"Well, I'm certainly not going to give it away. Rent is due next week."

"That's not funny."

"Trust me I'm not laughing. I over two months in arrears," she says hoping that in some way it would make Martin smile. Even just a little bit.

"That's not what I meant, and you know it," he tells her quite firmly and without a single hint of any smile.

"Oh, isn't it?" she asks.

"No."

"Well, exactly what do you mean then?" Wendy asks very inquisitively as Martin didn't hesitate in answering her.

"Look, you know that I'm married and have other commitments now. But I'll see what I can manage to give you every month if it helps you to stop doing this then that's got to be a good thing hasn't it?"

Wendy was flabbergasted by this offer, so much so that to begin with she didn't know what to say, particularly as she knew that Martin had meant every single word of what he just said. "Oh Martin… I… I don't quite know what to say."

"Don't say anything then, apart from you'll let me help you," he says to her with his eyes literally pleading with her to say yes.

"Look, Martin, it's a lovely gesture from you, it really is, but there's no way I can take any money of you."

"Why not?"

"Because you're a married man with a life of your own and with bills to pay. So, thank you, but no," she adamantly tells him.

"You needn't worry about that alright. Let me deal with it okay."

"No, Martin."

"Look, don't try and deny anything now. When we both looked at each other just a couple of minutes ago, we both knew that the feelings that we had back then are still here now. And we promised each other all those years ago that we'd look out for each other always. I meant that promise back then and I still mean it now. Probably even more. I've always had deep feelings for you Wendy ever since we first met, and I always will. Please, let me help you?" His words came exactly where she thought they'd come, and that was straight from the bottom of his heart. She felt herself becoming a little tearful but there was no way she was going to let that show now.

"Do you really want to help me, Martin?"

"Yes, of course."

"Then please just take me back to the street where I jumped into your car."

"You what!" exclaimed Martin in disbelief.

"Please, Martin, just do this one thing for me okay? Please?"

Even though, once again, she couldn't bring herself to look at him, he knew, that after all these years, she meant what she had just said to him.

"I know that you don't know this area very well. So, if you go left at the end of the road, then take the first right, that'll start you on the way back and I'll direct you as we go along," she says continuing not to look at him as all Martin could now do was start the engine, and begin driving away.

As instructed, he took the first left, followed by

24

the first right, which took them along a long main road which they both knew, if Martin had just turned around at the Industrial Estate and followed the same road back, they would be back at the same street in less than ten minutes. But this way, and without either one saying anything else for now, they knew that this was going to be a few more extra precious moments together which they may never have again.

"If you turn right here, we'll be back in Ivydale Street," she says.

Martin did as he was asked, he thought he recognised the turning and then the street as he deliberately slows right down and takes his time in pulling up in almost the exact same part of the kerb as well.

"Thanks for bringing me back Martin," Wendy began by saying. "You're were so close to finding that Tesco's you know. All you had to do was go right instead of left at the end of this street then second left, just on the edge of the main part of town, it's right in front of you," she says firmly looking in his direction. But Martin was too pre-occupied for the moment writing something down on a scrap of paper.

"Take this," he says somewhat forcing it into the palm of her hand.

"What is it?" she asks.

"It's my mobile number," he tells her.

"Martin, we've just been through this. You're married, got a home and a whole other life to think about and for the last time I will not be accepting any money from you okay."

"Look, even if you don't want any money from me, just text me to let me know that you got home safely tonight okay. Please. Just for old times, sake."

They both gaze into each other's eyes again as Martin this time fought the urge to throw his arms around her and kiss her once again. But not half as much as Wendy fought to do exactly the same thing.

"Take care of yourself, Martin. And don't forget the teabags and Victoria sponge," she then says getting out of the car and leaving Martin disappointed that there wasn't at the very least a goodnight kiss on the cheek.

She was soon on the other side of the road and she turns her head around and watches Martin drive away and turn right at the end of the street. She was glad he did, knowing that he was on his way home to the life that she always believed suited him right down to the ground. But she was also happy that she had his mobile number safely tucked away in her jacket pocket. Just in case.

2

Not for the first time within the last thirty minutes, it was another look through the living room curtains, and yet again, all that could be seen was an empty driveway, which brought another sigh of anxious frustration. No sense in looking out at nothing, so Vanessa closes the curtains and turns and looks up at the wall clock and as she does so, the second hand appeared to be taking an eternity to travel around the clockface. It appeared that time had stood still at ten minutes to the hour and she finds it exceedingly difficult to believe that time could travel so slowly. But a check on her mobile phone confirmed that the clock was indeed correct as she is nervously tapping the screen as it wasn't like him not to at least phone to say where he was or how much longer he would be. She didn't like this. Maybe something bad had happened to him.

She rushes into the kitchen and once again checks that the cups and plates were already to go. Which they were but she also couldn't fail to notice that one of the plates had what appeared to be some specs of tomato sauce around its edge. And that just wouldn't do. That wouldn't do at all. So, it was quickly over to the sink and under the hot water tap and with just a squirt of washing up liquid and sponge as she carefully washed all the specs away to have the plate all clean and shiny again and with a wipe of tea towel it was placed back amongst the other plates before going back into the living room, looking back up at the wall clock, now it was only nine minutes to the hour. "Where is he?" she asks

It was like she had just said 'abracadabra' as a car was then heard coming up the driveway. Like a gazelle, she sprung across the living room to the curtains and threw then open as a huge smile if relief appears across her face as her husband was now safely home. It didn't matter that he'd been gone for nearly three hours just to buy a couple of items, he was now home. That's all she cared about for now.

"Where did those last four minutes go?" she couldn't but wonder as for no particularly reason she finds herself glancing at the clock again and another check on her mobile confirmed that the film was due to start in five minutes.

"Christ, is it that time already?" Martin says as, not forgetting what he went out to buy, gets out of the car, but suddenly remembering that he'd also bought an extra treat of a chocolate éclair each for them, especially as he knew that his wife was a big fan of them as he heads into the marital home. "I'm home!" he calls out the very second, he enters before closing the front door behind him.

"In the kitchen!" he hears in answer and that's exactly where he heads just as quick as he can and on arriving, he's so happy to see his wife stood there waiting for him, but not half as happy as she was to see him.

"You're home at last," she starts by saying. "I was really getting worried about you, especially when I phoned and you didn't answer."

"I know, I know, I'm so sorry about that. It took me ages to eventually find that Tesco's Metro. God only knows how many times I got lost in the process. I must have driven around the town at least three times. And it's not that I don't appreciate the present, because I really do, but I've got to find someone who can look that sat nav. It sent me the wrong way so many times, I thought I was going to end up in China or somewhere like that," he explains to her as she then jumps in to say.

"I phoned you a little while ago. I was getting worried."

"Yes, I know that you did. But my phone had fallen onto the floor and ended up somewhere under my seat and I was driving at the time. I probably should have phoned you after I'd been to the shop, but once I knew where it was, I just thought that I'd get back here pronto. Which is what I did." He tells her with an innocent face which, to his deep-down complete surprise, he found quite easy to do, as their relationship up to this very point had never heard a single lie from either one of them. Not even a little white one. But he knew that he couldn't keep up this innocent expression for too much longer as the guilt that he now felt could so easily surface, as the kettle clicked to signal that it was now boiled.

"Oh well, I suppose these things happen," Vanessa begins saying as deep-down Martin was giving a sigh of relief as she starts taking the little bit of shopping out of his hands as suddenly she notices the eclairs. "Oh lovely," she then says.

"Yeah, thought they'd make a nice little extra treat for us. Well for you really," he says as Vanessa's eyes clearly indicated that he had done well.

As she makes the tea, he cuts up the Victoria

Sponge, gathers all the plates especially not forgetting the little side plates just for the eclairs and, adjourning to the living room, the romantic in Martin rose to the surface as he dimmed the lights before he joined his wife on the sofa in perfect timing as the film which they planned to watch together all week, had now just started.

It may not have been The Ritz with champagne and caviar, but it suited these two perfectly, especially Vanessa, she turns and looks adorningly at her husband as he takes a bite out of his slice of cake. Out of the corner of his eye, he notices her looking, he smiles at her before planting a kiss gently upon her lips, which pleased her immensely.

"Thanks. What was that for? Not that I'm complaining you understand," she says.

"No reason really. Just because we're here, together," Martin says which Vanessa thought was a good answer before they both turn to the television.

"I've always liked this film. Think I fell in love with it from the very first time that I watched it," she says.

"Must admit, never been much of a one for rom coms as well you know. But this one is a bit different. It's clever. Especially where all the stories sort of link together at Heathrow at the end," he says.

"Oh yeah, I like that as well," says Vanessa taking a sip of her tea as Martin then continues.

"And they're some good actors in this as well. I mean look at Bill Nighy there singing. He's great, and he plays the part of an aging rock star perfectly."

"Yeah, that's right he does. Hugh Grant makes me laugh as well. Especially when he starts dancing around No.10," she says as they both start laughing at the thought of it. "And isn't it lovely near the end when that, oh what's his name, Colin Firth that's it, when he goes over to Portugal at Christmas when he's supposed to be spending it with his family to propose to that girl. Don't see you doing anything like that for me," she says giving him a friendly nudge.

"Well, do you live in Portugal?" he asks.

"No."

"Right, do you even speak Portuguese?"

"Well, obviously not," she says.

"Right, so there you are then. I won't be doing anything like that will I?" he says as Vanessa then gives him a playful slap on his arm before he then says. "But I did go out for nearly three hours just to make sure that you got your cake and eclairs for an extra treat. Surely that must count for something?"

"Oh, you're my real knight in shining armour aren't you eh," she says as they share one more quick kiss before turning their attention fully to the film.

They laughed when it was funny. They went Aww when it was romantic. And they somehow both felt the exact same pain as the actors in the sad parts. And once the film had ended, and all the cake, and eclairs had been eaten, they both sat back in each other's arms with a feeling of such contentment, that neither one wanted to move a single inch and they could have easily settled there for the rest of their lives as Martin eventually remarked.

"Ahh, this is so lovely, what a great night this has been."

Vanessa couldn't have put it any better herself before he goes on to say, "And let's hope for many, many more like them."

"Yeah, I'm sure that there will be because I'm so happy right now Martin. Don't want any of it to end," Vanessa tells him with the puppy dog eyes that she can do so well. And which Martin could never resist. No matter how hard he tried at times.

"Neither do I," he says as not for the first time tonight, he gazed into a pair of now twinkling blue eyes, only this time it was different. It wasn't just a case of strong feelings which had been buried and almost forgotten and were now returning. These eyes were saying how much she loved him.

"There's only one thing that we need to make this marriage complete," Vanessa says as she gently begins patting her stomach. Martin didn't have to say anything, he just nodded, as he knew exactly what she was referring to.

"Do you think that it'll work this time?" she asks with hope literally pouring out of her eyes which Martin, for now, had absolutely no intention of dashing.

"Yeah, of course. Why shouldn't it work for us? We're both decent people with good morals who love each other very much and I'm going to stay one million per cent positive about this okay." He gave her so much hope and optimism, that Vanessa felt right now that anything was possible. But it was only to last a few short moments as the reality in her came to the surface.

"But what if it doesn't, Martin, huh? What then? Not sure that I could take that sort of rejection again." Martin just threw both his arms around her.

"Look, even if it is a rejection, we keep going, alright. It's as simple as that. We keep trying and trying, no matter how much it costs or even if it might still happen naturally one day. I mean, you hear stories all the time of women being six or even seven months pregnant and not having a clue that they are.

Christ, some have even given birth without realising that they're pregnant. So, we should never give up. Because you'll be the best mum that any kid could ever wish to have."

Vanessa couldn't help but blush on hearing this compliment from the man that she loved so much. "Reckon you'll make a pretty good dad yourself," she begins by saying. "And you're so right, we must keep thinking positive about it as one day, it will happen for us."

"Exactly," Martin says as without warning, Vanessa plants a kiss directly onto his lips. "Wow, thanks for that," he says very pleasantly surprised.

"You're welcome."

"Tell you what. Why don't you get yourself up to bed, and I'll clear everything up down here?" Martin offers.

"Are you sure. I don't mind staying and helping out, I'll even do it myself if you want," Vanessa say.

"No, honestly, I'll do it, won't take me too long to do."

"Okay then, if you're sure?"

"Yeah of course."

"Alright then if you insist. Must be honest I fancied a quick shower before getting into bed anyway. So, if you really don't mind, I'll pop up now then," Vanessa says as she quickly stands up and goes to leave, but before she passes through the doorway she turns back to Martin. "You won't be too long, will you?"

"I won't, I promise," he says smiling away as she makes her way up the stairs and straight into the bathroom.

He then takes all the dishes from the living room into the kitchen and put them straight into the sink and began washing and drying, before putting them all back into the correct cupboards, and with one final look around, satisfied it was all clean and tidy, he turns out the light and goes straight back into the living room. He quickly checks that all the windows are shut before switching off the television and after one quick, and satisfied look around, he switches the lights off before he heads towards the front door when he suddenly hears from upstairs. "Martin, have you finished?"

"Yeah, just locking the front door now," he calls back up to Vanessa who heads straight into the bedroom, a happy woman. He puts the safety chain across and checks that it's firmly secured before standing at the bottom at the stairs and just stands looking up. There was a woman just up those stairs who loved him dearly and would do anything to make him and this marriage as happy as she possibly could. That thought did without question make his heart virtually burst with happiness as what more he could ever wish for. But that still didn't stop him from checking the inbox on his mobile phone which, for now, showed no new messages. He wasn't too disappointed or indeed surprised by this, but that still didn't stop him being worried as he heads up the stairs turning the last of lights off.

3

Even though they were made of a thick material, dark red in colour and fully drawn, there was still enough light coming into this small bedroom to show the scattering of a woman's clothes over the floor, which mainly consisted of woman's sexy lingerie. The only form of what could be classed as sensible clothing was a pair of jeans that had been carelessly thrown over what looked like a cheap second-hand wooden chair. The borderline overflowing ashtray felt right at home on the floor amongst all this mess as Wendy began to slowly stir from her sleep.

It took quite a while for her to finally lift her head from under the duvet, but when she did and saw all the mess, she clearly wished that she hadn't and without hesitation, put her head right back under the duvet for now.

But now she had risen from under her duvet, it was virtually impossible for her to now go back to sleep, so she just lay on her back and stared aimlessly at the ceiling. Totally despondent, wondering what, and where it had all gone wrong. Her bedside cabinet was just as cheap looking as her chair, probably second-hand as well, with its mustard-yellow coloured paint flaking away and sitting on it, was a memory of far happier times. A photo of a much younger her standing outside what was her little florist shop 'Wendy's Flowers'. The feeling of accomplishment and sheer joy and happiness clearly showed in this photo and it served as a constant source of inspiration.

"One day," she whispers looking at it one more time as a smile appears on her face. Now whether this was about the photo or she could see the scrap of paper with Martin's mobile number next to it, only she will know for certain.

She seriously didn't want to, but it was time for her to get up. It still took a good few minutes for to drag herself out from under the duvet, put on her dressing gown which narrowly avoided upsetting the ashtray, and stumbled out of her bedroom.

The rest of her council flat wasn't that much better to look at either. Particularly the kitchen which still had scattered carelessly all over the sides what remained of last night's, or maybe even the night before', portion of chips and paper with the dirty plates to match. Plus, the sink was full of cold and dirty dishwater with many cups just floating around aimlessly, none of which made for a bright and cheerful welcome to a brand-new day.

Despite the place looking far from welcoming and hospitable, Wendy still manages to find at least one clean cup for her first coffee of the day as she sat down at the kitchen table where there was some letters waiting for her. There was no way that she was going to open them without first taking a large sip of her coffee and lighting up her first cigarette and it was only then, that she found enough courage to open up the first one.

"Oh my god, that's scarily uncanny," she says somewhat jokingly, looking at the letter which was, as she said to Martin last night, a arrears notice for her rent, and as she also predicted, it was for two months and it also advised that she should phone the local council to discuss if she was having difficulty, about a payment method that would suit her to prevent this from happening again.

It just got discarded to one side for now, she just couldn't face it as the second one was then opened, which was hardly filling her with any hope that a long-lost relative had suddenly passed away and had left her a million-pound fortune to be collected immediately. And she was right as it was a final reminder of her credit card which she had completely forgotten about. This wasn't how she planned out her life to be. By now at this time of her life, she had always thought, like most normal people, that she'd be totally settled with a husband and children living in a nice area with good neighbours, living a normal and happy life. Not one of poverty and living in squalor. She couldn't help but shed a tear or two as she wondered what on earth to do next.

There was a knock at the door. It was ignored, as she was in no mood for visitors and just continued with her coffee and cigarette when she suddenly realises that there was no ashtray on the table. A quick glance to her right and there was a handily placed saucer on the side which would suffice for now as she could wash it later with all the rest of the cups in the sink that needed doing. There was a second knock on the door. It was greeted with the exact same response as the first. Coffee and cigarette remained the highest priority right now.

"Oi, Wendy, you up yet or what?" what sounded like a young man's voice coming through her letterbox then shouted and it was followed by yet another knock, only this time a much louder, and somewhat aggressive. Wendy just sighed heavily.

"Yeah alright I hear you," she mutters, stubbing out her cigarette and getting up to make her way towards her front door. Through the frosted safety glass, she could just about make out a figure of a man stood there, and she could hazard a good guess who it was. Which hardly filled her with any sort of joy.

"Bloody hell, you're not exactly a morning person, are you?" Chris says the very moment that the door was opened as he looked at Wendy thinking that he had just made some sort of clever remark. Wendy didn't think it remotely clever.

"What do you want, Chris?" she asks.

"You know very well what I want. But I wouldn't say no to a nice cup of tea while I'm here if there's one going. Which I think that there'll will be for me," he somewhat, what he thought, cheekily says.

"Well there isn't," Wendy tells him.

"Oh don't be like that, Wendy, you know that you love me really," he says barging his way through and finds his way straight into the kitchen. "See you don't believe in doing the dishes then!" he calls out as Wendy very reluctantly closes the door and goes into the kitchen.

There was a time, not all those many years ago,

that Wendy would in no way at all entertain a scruffy, baseball cap wearing layabout, who hadn't, or never even intended to do an honest day's work in his life. Choosing instead to go around and pretend to be some sort of wannabe gangster. Pathetic. That's what Wendy often thought of him. But these days, things were so different that she unfortunately had to tolerate him.

"And before you ask, no sugar for me, 'cause I'm sweet enough," he begins by saying, still thinking that he was clever or even funny. "Oh, come on, Wendy, give us a smile eh."

But the last thing that she wanted to do is smile or even break out into a small grin as she just didn't want to encourage him and just carried on with making the tea.

"What happened between you and that Tanya bird last night then?" he asks keen to know.

"What do you mean?"

"Well she's saying that you took some punter from right under her nose last night?"

"You what?"

"Yeah apparently, well so she's been saying, that she was negotiating a price with this bloke and you just jumped in the passenger side of his car and he drove off with you in it. She wasn't at all happy about it," he says quite admiring the fact that she actually had the nerve to do such a thing.

Wendy had only one answer. "Tough luck if she didn't like it. She would have done the same to anyone else," she says passing Chris his tea and having another coffee for herself.

"Okay, yeah, you're probably right about that. Anyway, bit flash was he. Plenty of dosh was it, good payer," Chris asks hungry to know more.

"None of your business," she tells him point blank.

"Oh c'mon, Wendy, no need for that. What happened eh. Bit kinky or something was he? Or did he like it rough? He asks giving a dirty little chuckle as he was clearly thinking about all sorts of sexual pleasures that she just may have had to perform last night. It amused him. Which Wendy could tell, with this and now along with the sight of his yellow-stained-gapped teeth prominently showing, it was more than enough to make her feel physically sick.

"Like I said, it's none of your business, alright," she says, which made it perfectly clear to Chris that this subject was now closed.

"Fair enough," he says taking a large sip of his tea. "Tell you what though Wendy, you do make a good cup of tea. You can't clean for shit I mean, have you never heard of washing up liquid. And I bet your front room has forgotten what a hoover feels like. But in saying that, with a bit of training, I reckon you'd make someone a good wife one day. Failing that though, you could always come work for me. You're still a pretty woman no denying that, so with your looks and my brains and connections, we could make a nice few quid together. I'd look after you. You could be my top girl."

Wendy had only used violence in recent years purely as a form of defending herself, but the urge just to lash out and hit him with the nearest heavy object, like that dirty frying pan, which was next to the sink, was very, very strong indeed for what he had just said. The only reason that she didn't was probably because she would be very unlikely just to stop at one hit.

"Anyway, I didn't just come here for a cuppa and a chat, did I?" He says winking at her, and she knew exactly what he meant by that. Her purse was where she remembered she left it last, on top of the refrigerator. After opening it, she counts out exactly what was required and begrudgingly, as she could really use this money for her bills right now, hands it over to Chris who, not caring in the slightest if it appeared to be rude or untrustworthy, quickly checked it himself.

And once he had done, he looked menacingly at her. "It's short," he says.

"No, it's not," Wendy insists.

"It is," he says a touch more insistent.

"No, it's not."

"I'm telling you…" he didn't get a chance to say anymore as Wendy jumped right on him.

"And I'm telling you, there's one hundred and fifty quid there, as we agreed, alright! Now that's me and you even, alright! We're quits!"

Normally in this situation, namely mostly girls that are a lot younger than him, Chris wouldn't think twice about using more intimidating tactics to get what he wants. But seeing how Wendy was a grown woman who was in mood to be argued with, he thought better of it.

"Alright, alright Wendy, I was only joking with you. I know it's all there really, just as you said it was. I knew that you wouldn't let me down, and you haven't," he says as Wendy promptly tells him. "I always pay what I owe."

"Like I just said, only joking with you. Never doubted you for a second, that's why I helped you out," he says finishing of his tea. He didn't think for a moment that one more dirty cup in the sink would make much of a difference as he just threw it in, it wasn't as if he was going to wash any of them. "Thanks again for the tea Wendy, nice it was. Sure, you won't change your mind about working for me. We'd be a good team me and you."

"No," Wendy was adamant.

"Right, but before I shoot off, can I interest you in some gear. Can get whatever you want. Bit of coke, smack, whatever you want. Do you a good deal as well," he says hoping for some sort of sale, but Wendy remained totally adamant.

"Look, you helped me out, and I'm grateful, but now you've been paid back get this through your head. I've never had or ever will touch any kind of drug and I've always got by without a pimp. I can take care of myself."

He makes a point of quickly showing her the money that she has just repaid him before putting it in his pocket as he takes a final look around the kitchen and gesturing to her with his eyes that she should take a closer look at the mess her kitchen was currently in as he then somewhat sarcastically says to her. "Yeah, of course you can." As he then leaves.

She was relieved to finally see him go. Hopefully, she won't have to have any more dealings with him in the future. Taking a moment to think about what he said as he left and the sarcastic tone it was said in, she couldn't help, no matter how much it hurt her to do it, to admit that he was right. Things needed to be addressed in her life, like proving what she had just said to Chris that she can indeed look after herself, and the best way to prove that to begin with, would be to start with cleaning up her flat. As this wasn't the person she really was, she'd never lived like this before, ever, and she wasn't going to any longer.

Once the coffee was drunk and the cigarette smoked, there was no putting this off any longer. The sink was as good a place to start as any, as she threw the saucer she had been using as an ashtray in amongst the dirty cups. The cleaning up took longer than she thought but she felt a small sense of achievement by completing it, which included throwing away the remains of the Chinese Takeaway, wiping down all the kitchen sides. The mood to tidy was now flowing stronger that it had had for weeks and it was straight into the living room to clear away any rubbish and put all her letters and bills safely away in a draw under the television with some old DVD'S and then the hoover made a rare appearance from behind the sofa and she went around the entire flat, not forgetting to dust and polish where she could, like a woman clearly on a mission, not just to clean, but to start taking some more control back in her life.

"There, that's a bit better," she says putting the hoover back behind the sofa as she looked around her entire flat, admiring her handywork, looking and feeling quite pleased with herself as it would do for her for now. It wasn't as if anyone else was going to see it anytime soon as she never even thought of bringing a punter back here to her home. And never would.

Thinking of punters, it was almost time to start to think about working tonight. But she wasn't going anywhere without something to eat so it was back to the kitchen to first check the cupboards. But apart from coffee and teabags, they were bare. Not even a single biscuit was to be seen. The fridge only had a half full bottle of tomato sauce but thankfully the freezer did have tucked away in the bottom tray, half a packet of frozen steak cut chips, which were luckily for her still well in date. So, it was in the oven they went and at least she had some tomato sauce to go with them as she sat down with a coffee and it wasn't hard to see that the hunger had really got hold of her as she demolished the entire plateful in no time at all, and after ensuring that all the dishes were done and packed away properly again, it was time for a shower and to begin to getting ready for work.

She always despised what she found herself ended

up doing for a living, which was why she took just as long as was humanly possible in there to prolong the agony of yet another night of it. Then it was into the bedroom to look through her wardrobe to decide what would look good on her tonight.

Well thigh high black boots and fishnets are usually popular with a lot of men and they did seem to suit her legs well. Leather or denim? Leather or denim? It was usually a tricky dilemma to see which type of mini skirt would look better. Eventually it was leather that won and with a tight red top and leather jacket which now sort of chose itself and as she laid it all out on her bed, in her newly cleaned bedroom, she thought to herself, "That will do for tonight."

She sits at her mirror and just like in the shower, takes her time in drying her hair and applying her make-up. Blue eye shadow always seemed to go down well, not too much foundation, but the deep red lipstick was a must. And when she was finally ready for another night, she looked at herself in the full-length mirror on her wardrobe door. There was no doubting that even though she was far from being a teenager anymore, she still had maintained her looks. It was just a pity that she had to totally rely on them now just to get by. She wasn't quite ready to go out yet.

To begin with it wasn't quite dark yet and even though it wasn't a secret to almost everyone in the block where she lived what her current occupation was, there was no need to advertise the fact by going out in broad daylight. She sat in her recently cleaned kitchen at the table with just one more coffee and cigarette, this time she'd found an ashtray to use, and look out of her window watching day ever so surely becoming night. It didn't take too long for the darkness to cover the entire town and looking at a half moon, she knew it was time to go. It was just one more quick check that she had everything. Keys, handbag, cigarettes which she was running low on, mobile phone and purse, which she looked inside of and saw her last remaining ten pound note, and she couldn't get through without her cigarettes so that was where that was going as she hoped and prayed that it was going to be a profitable night for her. Because it so needed to be as turning off the lights, she made her way out of the safety of her nice clean flat and walked into the total unknown.

It was common for Wendy to get the odd wolf whistle as she walked out on her estate. Mostly from the old man who lived on the ground floor by himself and had done for almost ten years since his wife died. She always saw the funny side to this as he looks through his opened kitchen window and even sometimes blows Wendy a friendly kiss, which she always kindly returned as it always made his night.

"How are you Ronnie?" she asks.

"I always feel good when I catch a sight of you, Wendy. You make me wish I was at least twenty years younger because I'd be chasing you all over this block," he says laughing.

"Tell you what, Ronnie, if you were twenty years younger, I wouldn't be running away from a handsome devil like you," she says laughing in return, which really made Ronnie's night even better.

"Take care Wendy love," he says with a cheery wave goodbye closing his kitchen window as feeling the cold.

"I will, Ronnie, love," she says waving goodbye to him as she continues walking along the quiet street for about ten minutes or so, ensuring that her jacket was done up properly to keep out the cold night air.

The need for cigarettes became even more evident as on checking her packet she was down to her last three which was in no way going to last the night and it was straight into the oncoming shop. On entering, and even though it was way beyond her budget for now, she did wanders up the aisle where all the wine and spirits were kept and thought to herself how nice it would be just to have a nice bottle of Chardonnay and be sat at home in front of the TV. That's with or without a man. But for now, it was just her cigarettes and just enough for a packet of chewing gum.

It wasn't long after that she was back in Ivydale Street. It was deserted for now as Wendy cut a solitary figure walking slowly up and down and it was no big surprise that there weren't many people out on another cold night like this. But Wendy soon spotted, coming down on the other side of the road, a young man looking distinctly sheepish. Nervous even. As he couldn't help but keep looking at her which Wendy couldn't fail to notice. "You alright love?" she says to him.

This clearly spooked the young man and made him feel more nervous than he already was as he tried avoiding any sort of eye contact with her, but he wasn't fooling Wendy. She knew what he wanted, but he was obviously too terrified to ask. So, taking the bull by the horns, she crosses the street goes straight up to him. "You alright there, love? You lost or something?"

Wendy thought that she may have scared this young man enough to give him a heart attack judging by the way he almost jumped out of his skin.

"Easy there darling. I'm not going to hurt you or anything," she says kindly which gives the young man a touch of reassurance as he sorts of smiles at her. "There you see, don't bite do I love. What's your name?"

Even though it was dark, Wendy could clearly see that the young man beginning to blush. He was blushing so much that he gave a little bit of heat which she was grateful for as stood closer to him. "Aww bless you darling. No need to be embarrassed around me. C'mon, calm yourself down tell me your name?" Her kindness began to have some effect on this young man as he slowly said.

"Gary. My name is Gary."

"There you go, see, didn't hurt did it? It's nice to meet you Gary, I'm Wendy. Do you smoke?"

"Erm, yeah, yeah I do," he tells her as then even though his hands were shaking due to nerves and not the cold, he takes out a packet of cigarettes from his coat pocket and happily gives one to her. He went to light it for her as well, but he was still shaking so much she thought that he might just set her hair on fire on something.

"Easy there Gary love, don't panic I'll light it myself alright, but thanks anyway," she says gently pushing his lighter to one side and getting her own out of her handbag and lighting up. "So then Gary, what brings you down here tonight?" It took him a good minute or two to answer, but he did.

"Well, I don't want to be rude, but are you, well, you're a…"

Wendy cut him off there. "Yes, Gary I am. But I'm sure that a good-looking lad like you has no real need for someone like me. You should be out somewhere with your girlfriend."

"Erm, well, I haven't got a girlfriend," he begins by saying before he really stutters out. "I've never had one, ever."

"Oh, I see. So, you've never," Wendy says as Gary shakes his head almost too embarrassed to say the actually word.

"Oh, Gary, love, there's no need to be embarrassed, it can happen to anyone alright. So, that's why you're down here tonight." He just nods still feeling the embarrassment.

"Like I said Gary daring, this can happen to anyone, don't worry about it. Right, it'll cost you fifty quid, sorry about that but I do have bills to pay, you understand that don't you? Right, you got a car?" Wendy asks getting down to the business, which she just had to do.

"Yeah, I'm parked just around the corner," Gary tells her.

"Good boy. Now its money up front. Is that okay

with you love?"

"Yeah, that's fine," Gary says reaching into his pocket and counting out the money which Wendy was incredibly grateful to see but before she had a chance to touch any of it.

"Oi you! what are doing back her again!" Both Wendy and Gary look across the street to see a terribly angry Tanya now beginning to make her way across the street towards them both, and she was not alone. As a large, rough, burly looking man was walking next to her, Wendy surmised that it was her pimp and they both approached just her as by now Gary decided that this was clearly nothing to do with him.

"What are you doing back down here again? You've got a bloody nerve after what you done to me last night!" Tanya rants and raves at Wendy before the man then asks.

"Is this the one, Tanya?"

"Yeah, this is her, Dazza," Tanya tells him, he then looks directly at Wendy. Not at all pleased with her.

"Right, listen to me you, Tanya and only Tanya works this street got that! And anyone else who wants to work here must go through me to get permission and to arrange my cut. Is that clear?" He says clearly meaning everything single word.

"That's right, you thieving bitch! This is my street got it!" Tanya says shoving Wendy which she didn't take at all lightly and pushes her right back.

"Firstly, you keep your hands to yourself, secondly, I don't see any signs around here with your name on it saying this is your street and thirdly, if you really want to fight me over who works here then fine! I got no problem with that! But he stays out of it, right!" Wendy says more in desperation for money than actual bravery and stood there all set to defend herself from anything that Tanya would throw at her. The last thing that she wanted though was for any form of violence to occur, even though she had now thrown her jacket to the ground in readiness for it as she turns to Dazza.

"Look, Dazza, mate, c'mon, there's no reason why we can't both work this street tonight. Me on one side her on the other and I promise that I won't cross over if she doesn't, yeah. I'll even work for you tonight eh, fifty-fifty, straight down the middle can't say fairer than that can I? Come on, you're a businessman, surely you must see that two lots of money is better than one. Please, come on, I've got bills that seriously now need paying. Let me work, yeah." Tanya then screams.

"No bloody way are you working here tonight you nasty cow!" as was just about to lunge at her as Wendy was now set to defend herself from her.

But she wasn't expecting to defend herself from a right hook Dazza then threw at her.

"Don't you ever touch Tanya, you bitch!!" He yells right at Wendy who was still reeling from that punch to her face. But she didn't have time to recover from it as Dazza just laid into her again and again with a left then a right all connecting cleanly to her face, and she was soon on the floor with blood coming from her mouth and nose and the start of what would appear to be a huge black eye.

"Do you want a go, Tanya?" Dazza asks.

"Too right I do," says Tanya, as then taking great pleasure in first kicking her twice in the stomach, before going around and stamping her heels into her back, Dazza, who seemed to be getting some perverse kick out of this, grabs Wendy by the her collar and unleashes one more right, followed by a left straight into her face and even though these last two punches were to put specks of her blood onto his what looked like a brand new white parka coat, he was now relentless, as mercilessly he was going for a least one more on a battered and by now heavily bloodied Wendy when out of nowhere police sirens were heard coming down the street.

"Come on move!" shouts Tanya as she grabs a hold of Dazza's arm. They both flee into the night at the sight of the police car who just pulls up on the kerb, not really bothering to chase them, as the two officers were more concerned with Wendy, who was a bloody mess laying on the freezing cold pavement. The first officer immediately put on a pair of latex gloves and did all that he could for Wendy who could hardly speak by now as the second officer made sure that an ambulance was called.

"Hello, can you hear me? What's your name?" The first officer asks but Wendy was dazed, practically unconsciousness unable to answer. "What was that all about then eh? Over who's turf this was, over a punter or both eh love? Come on, what happened here, tell me?" But again, Wendy was unable to answer, she was in too much agony, but thankfully for her the ambulance was soon to arrive and take her away to be treated properly with one of the officers escorting all the way to hospital.

4

It's not that she wasn't grateful. She was extremely grateful for all what had been done for her. But it was time for Wendy to leave, she had to. Despite all what the doctor was telling her about the concussion that she had suffered last night, but there was just no way in making her see sense right now.

"Alright, if you insist but please, you must come straight back to A&E, the first sign of an headaches or any other pain and discomfort," the doctor says to Wendy, literally pleading for her not to go anywhere just yet.

"Thanks doc for all you've done for me, I do appreciate it, honestly I do, but it's time that I wasn't here," Wendy says through her still black and blue battered face and she tried in vain to disguise the wince that she gave as her ribs were in pain yet again.

"You're in no fit state to leave," the doctor says as

she clearly noticed that her ribs were hurting her, and she knew that it won't be the last time she feels that pain in the near future. Despite the bandages.

"Honestly, doctor, I'll be okay," Wendy insists again but the doctor was not at all convinced, but she was powerless to stop her leaving.

"Okay, very well, but I'm telling you that you can't go back to work for a least a week, possibly two," the doctor says but again, Wendy was not going to listen.

"Doctor, that isn't going to happen. Got bills to pay, you know what I mean." The doctor looked almost at the end of her tether with Wendy now.

"Your health must come first otherwise you'll soon be a total wreck and then where will you be?" Wendy knew only too well that what she was saying made perfect sense, but her current predicament dictated otherwise.

"Doctor, I'm self-employed, and on my own, and these bills need paying." The doctor reluctantly had to give up on her as there was no way Wendy was going to listen to her.

"Alright, but at least give yourself twenty-four hours or, even better, forty-eight hours to rest up, please." Was the doctor's last plea to her.

"I'll do my best doctor, I promise," Wendy says but as far as the doctor was concerned, not exactly convinced that she meant a single a word of what she just said as Wendy then not only made her way of the ward, but out of the hospital, still with her now dirty clothes from last night on and her prescription for the painkillers.

"Well at least it's not raining," she says to herself lighting up a much needed cigarette, standing outside the main entrance, not looking like she was in a great hurry to move anytime as soon as she took a look at her prescription and turns and looks and the nearby hospital pharmacy, wondering whether she should collect her painkillers now. But with no money on her, that hardly seemed a viable option.

A paramedic who then walked past her couldn't fail to spot the black thigh-high boots and fishnet stockings, which he seemed to like the look of very much. Wendy spotted him in an instant no matter how hard he tried to be discreet about it. "What time does your shift finish love, I'll come back and meet you here if you want, bit of fun, y'know what I mean," Wendy says giving him a wink as, in a flash, he turns his head away and he couldn't get into the hospital quick enough to spare his blushes which did give Wendy some momentarily pain relief.

"Excuse me madam, but you're only supposed to smoke at the shelters provided," a male voice sounding very much in authority then tells Wendy, who was not in any mood to listen to some Jobsworth, and was all set to say so as she turns and gets a much needed pleasant surprise as it was in fact Martin stood there who had just mimicked a different voice. Inside, she was literally jumping for joy at seeing him and the urge just to throw her arms around him, injured ribs or not, was almost too much to bear. But she managed to resist the urge and instead settled for a gentle smile.

On the other hand, Martin, even though initially pleased to see that she had been released from hospital, got quite a shock, his jaw fell open, to see her huge black eye on one side with the other looking bloodshot and swollen, just her bruised cheeks and the cut on her lip quite clearly would not be going away anytime the near future. Not really knowing what to say right now, Wendy thought it best to try and put him at ease. "It looks a lot worse than it really is. Honestly, Martin, I'm okay."

"Are you sure about that? Because I've got to be honest with you, you don't look it," Martin eventually says.

"I'll survive this, promise you I will. Anyway, you should see the other guy." Martin most definitely did not see the funny side to this and was in no way about to join Wendy in smiling about the whole thing which she could easily tell as she changes her put-on happy expression, for a far more serious one. "I'm sorry if I bothered you Martin, truly I am, but I literally had no one else to turn to. Look, I just need a lift back to my place that's all. If you can do that for me I'd be grateful."

"You done the right thing contacting me, so don't worry about that alright. You going to tell me what happened to you?"

"Don't want to talk about it just now, Martin, if that's alright. Can we just go now?" she asks as in return he asks.

"You had any breakfast yet?" Martin could very easily surmise from her lack of an answer. "I'll take that as a no then. Right, come on, I know a half-decent café not too far from here."

"Yeah, that sounds okay but just as long as you're sure because like I said I only want a lift home."

"Of course, I'm sure, just said so didn't I?" he says leading her towards his car. It wasn't too much later that they were pulling up outside a nearby café which Wendy didn't look entirely thrilled to see.

"Look, it's not that I'm not grateful, because I really am, but do you think that we could go somewhere else Martin?"

"Why, what's wrong with this place?"

"Just don't like this place, never really have, food's not that great either." Martin looked a touch suspiciously at her.

"You okay? Look, don't worry about money. I'm paying for this. Bit hungry myself now, could do with a full English with a nice couple of rounds of toast to go with it."

"It's not, Martin." He looks at her a touch puzzled by her reluctance to go in and after a minute's thought, he thought he knew the reason why.

"Wendy, look, I get that it can't be easy for you, but just try and forget about the way you look right now. We'll find a quiet corner alright, out the way of everyone okay. C'mon, you must be hungry because I know for a fact that it isn't just my stomach rumbling. And if anyone dares to say a word or even stare at you, then they'll have me to deal with, alright."

He wanted nothing more than to help. Never mind who's stomach was now rumbling the loudest, all Martin could think of was helping Wendy like he always said he would. Even though she was still quite reluctant. "Okay, Martin, let's go," she says.

"There you go, that's the spirit," he says as he rushes out of the car and like a true gentleman, opens the passenger door for her and to say that Wendy was impressed by this act of chivalry, would be an understatement, as he takes a firm grip of her hand and leads her into the café.

It wasn't full by any means, but not exactly empty either as the customers just sat at their respective tables with their meals and drinks, all minding their own business.

"There you are Wendy," Martin begins by saying. "Told you that you had nothing to worry about." He spots a quiet table tucked away in the far corner and he thought that this would suit them both perfectly. But before either one of them had a chance to take their seats, from behind the counter, an unpleasant, tall, and noticeably big woman, literally screeches out across the entire café.

"Hey, you! What the hell do you think you're doing, huh? Don't you even dare of thinking of sitting down and get your scrawny dirty ass out of here right now or I'll personally come over there and kick you out! You dirty whore!"

This certainly made all the customers sit up and take notice as Martin could only stand glued to the spot looking at the woman who's almost blood-red expression wasn't just only from the hot kitchen that she was working in as her eyes refused to leave Wendy who looked a touch embarrassed. Not for herself, but for Martin.

"Come along, Martin, let's go somewhere else. There's another one not too far from here," she says trying to push him towards the door. But he wasn't having any of it.

"No, we're not going anywhere. We've done nothing wrong," he says to Wendy before turning to the woman behind the counter. "What's the matter with you? We haven't done anything wrong. All we done was come in and was about to take a seat."

The woman behind the counter though, was clearly in no mood to listen to any sort of reason.

"You listen to me you! If that nasty little tart isn't out of here within the next five seconds, I'm going to come over there and take great pleasure in grabbing her by the hair and then drag her out of here! Got that!"

All the customers deep down were hoping that Wendy refused to leave so that they could all have a good story to tell all their family, friends, neighbours, and even those down the pub tonight as Martin was all set to speak on Wendy's behalf again.

"Please Martin, it's just not worth it, alright. Trust me, let's just go." She finally manages to usher him out of the door and was all set to leave with him, much to the disappointment of all the customers.

"That's right, get out and stay out!" The woman shouts out, but Wendy just had to answer that.

"Listen to me you fat cow! If you were any sort of wife or woman, then maybe your husband wouldn't have to go with elsewhere! Especially with someone like me!" She then slams the door behind her leaving the woman behind the counter raging away while all the customers still may not have had a great story to tell everyone, but it wasn't a bad one either.

"Right, that's two full English, with extra mushrooms on both, with one brown bread toast and one white bread toast and a fresh mug of tea each and if there's anything else that you need just ask okay." The pretty young waitress says very pleasantly, smiling at them both. Which was a far cry from the reception they received at the other café and in addition to that, the food looked appetising.

"Tell you what, I'm so ready for this" Martin begins by saying just as the first fork full of baked beans found their way into his mouth and was then consumed. "Don't stand on ceremony Wendy, I know that you must be hungry. Go ahead and eat."

Wendy looked at Martin and seemingly she had been given the permission that she never needed to begin with, she began demolishing the food on her plate suggesting that even though she did have some steak cut frozen chips the night before, it clearly didn't fill any sort of gap in her obviously empty stomach.

Martin seemed to have guessed that for himself. "Bloody hell, you really need that don't you eh?"

Wendy suddenly stops eating and looks at him with somewhat pitiful eyes.

"Sorry. Totally forgot my manners there for a minute. Bit hungry. Sorry," she says.

"There's no need to be sorry for being hungry alright, you just enjoy it," Martin tells her with an understanding smile which made Wendy feel a lot more at ease. Just like he always could.

"Right, do you want to tell me how you ended up in hospital last night?"

"No, not yet," Wendy instantly replied not wishing to be rude, but she was just in no mood to talk about that just yet.

"Okay then, so what was that all about in the other café?" Martin asks as Wendy felt up for answering this one.

"I went with her husband which I suppose is bad enough, but when she caught us around the back of that café, needless to say, she was none too pleased. She went for me then, but her husband stopped her from doing anything to me. Which was nice of him, but he must have regretted it because she gave him a real hiding there and then. Poor bloke. But it was their marriage so none of my business and I left them to it."

"Oh well, suppose you're right. It's their business to sort out. So, seeing how we didn't talk for that long the other night, what else has been happening? Because if you don't mind me saying, you're obviously down on your luck," Martin said not wishing to appear rude or anything, but in the hope that she may just open to him.

"Does it show that much," Wendy says in a vain attempt to once again make light of the situation that she was in. But that was becoming even more difficult with every passing moment and the way that Martin was now looking at her, only the truth will do from her now.

"Well, it's just like I began telling you the other night. The only reason that I'm like this is because of my ex-husband who gambled everything away. The lot. The house, car, all our savings, even lost my business because I ended paying all the bills for the house. Just couldn't afford to keep it all up because of his gambling. He'd bet on anything that he could. The horses, greyhounds, football, and that was before he went into the casino where it was games like Roulette and Blackjack. And he could never just walk past a Fruit Machine, no matter where it was without putting a least one pound coin into it. Even if it was the last one at the time.

"Never forget the day that the Bailiffs came. Without a doubt that was the most humiliating day of my life. They took the lot. I couldn't bear to watch, so I just drove to a quiet spot miles from anywhere and from anyone who might just know me and I think that for the first time in my life, I cried. I mean properly cried. Had to give the car back a week later.

"My family all tried telling me about him. That if I stayed with him it will only lead to heartache. But of course, being in love, which I genuinely believed that I was, didn't listen to a single word that they said, no matter how hard or how many times they tried to tell me. I just wasn't having any of it. In the end they disowned me. Mum, Dad, Sister, and Brother. None of them will talk to me now after all the rows we had. Especially some of the things that I said which can never be taken back.

"I coped to begin with. After divorcing him I signed up with an Employment Agency and got myself into a shared house. That was okay. Shared with two blokes and one other girl, and they were all nice enough, but I wanted a place of my own, so I could get my life back on track the way I wanted it to be. It took a while but eventually I got myself a council flat. Alright, it may not be in the best area, but at least I was living by myself, which is what I really wanted to do, in order to get my mind in order and start sorting my life out.

"The Employment Agency, to begin with, always seemed to have a steady flow of work for me. Shop work mostly. But I did do some cleaning jobs when it was required as I tried to find something permanent and full-time which didn't seem to materialise, no matter how many I applied for. Gradually, the work from the agency began getting less and less until one day it dried up completely, and no matter how hard I tried, couldn't even get a job flipping burgers, said I was over-qualified would you believe. And I just couldn't bring myself to sign on at first. I've always worked and had my own money. I had my own business for Christs sake! Why should I go cap-in-hand to anyone?

"But the bills began piling up. And one day, I just had to swallow my pride. I had a lie in that morning. Made sure of that. Probably because I wanted to put it off for as long as I could. But eventually I dragged myself out. Made myself look as presentable as I could before heading down there.

"There's a park nearby the dole office, don't know if you know it? It has a bench just a walk into it facing the building. I just sat there for hours watching all kinds of people coming in out and of it. Mostly scroungers though and you didn't have to be Einstein to work out that many of them never have or even intended to work a day in their life. Felt sorry for the few genuine people who went in there. Honest people who had just been unlucky for some reason or another. That's when I decided that I couldn't go through with it. I just didn't want people feeling sorry for me.

"I stood up, left the park and just wandered around for what must have been hours, not exactly sure where I was going or what I was going to do. I just needed to be out to try and clear my head and think straight. It was dark when I found myself accidentally down Ivydale Street, I got lost, bit like you did the other night. Never even heard of the place before and I had no idea what it was like down there, to me it was just an ordinary empty street with The Sailors Arms, which I now know to be a right dive, at the end of it. Didn't feel right me being down there, not right at all. All I wanted to do was just get out of there and get myself back to my flat.

"How much do you charge?" I literally jumped ten

foot in the air when this man came out of nowhere and asked me that. "Sorry, didn't mean to frighten you my love," he then says. He wasn't a dirty old man or anything like that. Looked quite respectable, smartly dressed, and well-mannered but still the shock of what he just asked me didn't leave me for ages.

"I'm sorry, you've got me confused with someone else, I don't do this sort of thing," I told him, which he seemed disappointed to hear."

"Are you sure?"

"Yes, I'm sure."

"Look, I don't want much, just a bit of company for an hour or so. Maybe a kiss and a cuddle. I won't hurt you I promise," he said and I didn't care how genuine he was in that it wasn't going to happen and I started walking away.

"I've got one hundred and fifty pounds here. Just sit with me in my car for an hour or so. That's all I want," he says.

"Hundred and fifty quid. Couldn't help but think to myself that would cover the electric bill, get some food in, and finally get the catalogue paid off. I turned back and looked at him and couldn't figure who was more desperate. Me or him. I established some boundaries with him that there would no full intercourse and if he even tried I'd be gone like a shot straight to the police and have him for rape. He agreed, so then I did go to his car, parked a couple of streets away.

"Nice car it was. Some sort of BMW, so I got in. Len his name was. He was a nice man really, just lonely, so we just chatted and now and again I let him cuddle and even kiss me. And once, and I mean just the once, I let him have a bit of a grope. Well, he was paying hundred and fifty quid. Anyway, after about an hour or so and true to his word, he paid up and let me go and gave me his number and said that if I ever wanted to meet up again then he'd be more than happy to. I told him that this'll probably never happen again so it didn't feel right to take his number and we said our goodbye's, and that was it. Hundred and fifty quid for just over an hour's work.

"I honestly didn't intend going back because believe me even though there was no full sex involved, I still felt dirty and spent well over an hour in the shower to get myself clean. But a week later, still no work, and hardly a penny left, I found myself going down there again. Wasn't so much money as the first time and we'll leave it at that shall we. It was hard, won't lie to you and it's never got any easier, but hey, it's a job that I don't have any formal qualifications for and I'm my own boss again and who knows, just might be as rich as Lord Sugar one day, own television show, telling people that you're fired! That'll be a laugh won't it."

But no matter how much she now chuckled, Martin couldn't see why she thought it funny.

"Wendy, how can you laugh about all of this. You're broke and look at the state of you right now."

Wendy stopped chuckling and the look that she then gave Martin was quite clear. How dare he say anything like that to her as she slams her hand down on the table in anger.

"I laugh because I have to laugh alright! It's what gets me through the day sometimes and when I think of some of the things I've had to do just to survive and make sure that there is at least some food in my cupboard, because I mean it, don't you dare sit there in judgement over me. You ain't got no right to do that, I promise Martin you haven't, alright."

"Wendy, Wendy, please calm down, I'm not here to judge you okay. Honestly, I'm didn't mean to come across like that, I promise. I just found it hard to understand why you acted like that, that's all. I'm sorry, truly I am." If it had been anyone else but Martin, then no doubt she would have totally lost her temper and despite her injuries, she'd had stood up and fought tooth-and-nail to defend her actions, but she soon began calming down.

"I'm sorry Martin. Shouldn't have gone for you like that. Especially after what you've done for me so far today." Martin just nodded to say it was okay as Wendy's initial anger looked clearly to be turning to despair and fought with the ounce of strength that she had to stop her breaking down in floods of tears as she just had to ask something of Martin.

"Martin, please, I need to ask you something which I've never asked anyone else in my entire life and it's something that I'd never thought I would ask of anyone," she begins before taking a deep breath as this was probably the most difficult thing that she's ever had to ask in her lifetime. "Could you please lend me some money, whatever you are able to lend I promise you faithfully that as soon as I can, I mean it Martin, I will. You know I will."

Martin though, wouldn't even entertain that idea as he reached into his wallet and pulled some money out, quickly counted it, and passed it over to her.

"There's a hundred there okay, and don't even think about paying me back until you are firmly, and I mean firmly back on your feet and by that I mean you're on telly telling someone that they're fired. Alright."

They both smiled and quietly laughed as he made

sure that Wendy took the money by squeezing it tightly into her hand as she whispers from the bottom of her heart, "Thank you."

"Look, I'm not here to judge or patronise you okay. But I guessed you were having problems when you text me earlier. So, I'm also guessing now that seeing how you've asked me for money, you probably haven't got any food at home," he says confidently knowing he was right and Wendy gave him no indication to think different.

"Thought so. Right, come along eat up, let's go supermarket," he says finishing his meal with the last piece of bacon.

"Martin, look, I can't let you do that. You've done more than enough already okay. Plus, you got a wife and other bills to think of. Please, this'll be enough," she says but Martin wouldn't hear of anything different.

"Listen to me now. My marriage and what other bills I must pay has got nothing to do with this okay. This is me taking care of you alright. Just like you'd do for me."

Wendy wasn't prepared to argue with anything that Martin had just said. Because he knew that he was right and she would do the same for him as she finished her meal with the last sausage, and both finish their mugs of tea and they were of.

"You really don't have to do this Martin, you lent me some money, so I can get my own tomorrow or maybe the day after," Wendy says but Martin had already got the trolley and was all set to go. "I'll just get you a few basics alright, keep you going and you can use the money for bills or something," he says as Wendy knew there was no arguing with him, so she just as well follow him in.

He was honest with her and said that for now he could only afford a few basic things. Wholemeal bread, butter, cheese, milk, teabags, coffee, some pasta and couple of sauces, bacon, eggs, some sausages and cereal, but she was eternally grateful and as they walked around together despite her outwardly battered and tattered appearance and his smart casual look, she got the sense that this was meant to be as it felt so natural, but she knew that for now it was all a pipedream. He was married and she couldn't or wouldn't let herself forget that for now. Even when he bought her a packet of cigarettes which he threw in the carrier bag so she'd have to accept them, she couldn't ignore the wedding ring which he wore.

*

"Anyhow, I told her not to wear that jacket with that top, it'll make her look fat and I was right wasn't

I? I know, there's just no telling some people no matter how much you try to help," Vanessa says with her mobile seemingly glued to her ear and totally engrossed in the conversation. Sat in the back of the taxi the chatting flowed but she couldn't help but recognise the man putting some shopping into the back seat of the car she also thought looked very familiar. But she had no idea who the woman was he was talking to.

"Do you know something, Maggie, I could have sworn that I just saw Martin outside a supermarket taking to what, not being rude now, was quite a rough looking woman. But it couldn't be, he's at work... Yeah, I'll ask him tonight when he gets home, I've probably made a mistake, anyway, what are planning to wear for Caroline's birthday meal?"

"So, this where you're living, these days then," Martin says pulling up to the block of flats where Wendy was living and as he looked at them and at the surrounding area, he was glad that he was staying with his car for now, even though it was broad daylight.

"Yeah, this is my Buckingham Palace," Wendy says before turning to Martin. "I can't thank you enough for what you've done for me and I will pay you back every penny I swear I will."

Martin was clearly offended to hear this. "What

did we say a little earlier in the café? You pay me back when you're a TV Star okay."

They both smile at each other. A smile which suggested more than friendship, just like the other when they both knew that the original spark was most definitely still there.

"This area looks a bit rough, maybe I should make sure you get home safely," Martin suggests.

She was most certainly tempted, no doubt about that, but as she looks again at his wedding ring, she thinks better of it. "Thanks for the offer, you're still the gentleman aren't you? But it's daytime, I'm sure I'll be alright."

Martin was disappointed to hear this, but knew she was right to say what she did. "Look, you've got my number now, Wendy please, anytime you need anything, just give me a text or something and I'll see what I can do for you okay."

It was the most honest and sincere offer that she had heard in so many years that it almost brought a tear to her eyes, but she fought the urge to start blubbing in front of him and instead just gave a friends only kiss on the cheek for now.

"Promise you Martin, if I need you, I'll be in touch, honest okay, bye for now," she says and not forgetting her groceries, she waves goodbye, deep down wishing things were so different as Martin, without showing it, felt exactly the same. He still felt that he should have walked her back to her flat but, she had his number and now he had hers, just so in future, he could check to see if she was doing okay. Just as friends though.

5

Even though her ribs were still very sore and tender, and there was still a bit of a headache to contend with, Wendy was quite happy to wake up the next morning. Her spirits were higher now than they had been for quite some time. There was a renewed optimism flowing through her and she felt that there was, even though it might only be a glimmer, but there seemed to be hope for the future. Looking once again at the photograph next to her bed with her outside her florist's, and even though she was still in very real financial trouble, it just felt that it could be possible that once again, happiness in her life could be achieved. And that, was simply down to Martin.

It may only have been the price of a breakfast, some grocery shopping and hundred pounds in cash but it was the thought and gesture behind it all that made it feel like she had just won the lottery and restored her faith that there are still good people out there. Or to be more precise, there was someone good in her life apart from the thieves, liars and (in her own words) the sex-starved losers which are usually a daily occurrence.

The scrap piece of paper with his mobile number was still next to her photograph. It wasn't really needed for now as his number was now on her phone but just in case of any accident, it was put safely away in her drawer before, moving extremely gingerly, she shuffled herself out of bed.

What a difference waking up to a nice clean flat made. Particularly walking into a clean kitchen. It may have been another cold winter's day outside but inside, Wendy was positively glowing which in turn was keeping her warm. Her good mood was then increased again as for the first time in weeks, she could actually sit down and have some breakfast. Cereal and a piece of toast. Not knowing for certain what money would be coming into the flat next or indeed when it would, Wendy was thoughtful enough not to go overboard when it came down to the amounts that she would have, but that couldn't stop her having the feeling of being somewhat civilised again.

It was still going to have to be Poundland for two-for-one on things like Washing Up Liquid, the local

Premier Shop for their own brand Baked Beans as anything Heinz was still out of reach just for the moment. Powdered Milk as well for her tea and coffee and keep the fresh for her cereal for as long as possible and maybe the time had now come for her to seriously start considering buying Hand-Rolling Tobacco instead of her normal cigarettes. Or even give up the habit completely. Best though have another smoke before making any rash decisions on that one.

"Right, just some rent paid off, then some cleaning stuff," she says thinking aloud stubbing out her cigarette and then ensuring that the kitchen was left clean, it was in the shower before off to the bedroom where she sat down in front of her mirror and no matter how battered and bruised she looked, that was in no way now going to put her of living her life and doing what she had to do.

It took a while, a good couple of hours to be exact but, with the right amount of make-up, she finally managed to cover up her bruised cheeks. Thankfully as well, her blood-shot was now showing signs of recovery but sadly, there was nothing at all that could be done for her black eye, just like there wasn't much point in putting on any lipstick. So, the decision was made there and then that if she had to deal with it, then so can everyone else.

This was most certainly a day for jeans, proper trainers on her feet, woolly jumper and parker coat to keep herself warm and grabbing her handbag, purse and her bag-for-life which was always kept in the cupboard next to the sink, it was time to go out and face the world once again.

Walking towards the town centre and the local council offices, the looks that she got from certain people, was very noticeable. Virtually all of them couldn't help but be shocked when they first saw the extent of her injuries as Wendy was doing her utmost to keep her head held high which, the more looks that she got, was becoming increasingly more difficult, but, she was able to hold herself together and then entering the local council offices.

After being asked to take a seat in the waiting area, Wendy very soon remembered why it was she only came down here when it was absolutely necessary. She, in no way, had a single upper class bone in her body as there was no way in this world that anyone who knew just the slightest thing about her would class her as a snob of any kind, but this place, always had her thinking that this is what the Dole Office would look like, because no matter how brightly they painted the walls with what looked like a Sunshine or

Golden Yellow. And disregarding the large picture of a Tropical Paradise which instantly caught your attention hanging on the wall from the very second that you walked in, the whole room just felt grim. As just like the Dole Office, she felt this was going cap-in-hand, and the people here didn't help matters either.

Apart from the occasional genuine person who had fallen on hard times and just needed a bit of help, like that smart-casually dressed man sat two rows in front of her. But the youngish single mother with her three unruly kids, who she was quite happy to sit on her lazy ass reading her gossip magazine, and let them cause havoc, where no doubt from three different fathers who was sat only five seats away from her. And like the probably intentionally scruffy and rough middle-aged couple sat almost directly behind her who did nothing but moan and complain about everything and everyone one.

Totally out-of-the-blue, a security guard charges through the waiting room and into one of the offices where everyone suddenly hears a young man, baggy jeans, and baseball cap screaming obscenities and making all kinds of foul-mouthed threats towards the staff because he wasn't getting his council flat just yet and had to be physically restrained and then escorted of the premises.

She was pleased to be called next, knowing that she didn't have to be here for too much longer. And even more happy when the woman who was dealing with her accepted a payment of fifty pounds from her now with a new arrangement set in place for future payments. Even though it was more than likely done out of sympathy for her.

"Right, fifty quid left, Poundland," she says standing outside lighting up a cigarette which, despite the cold air, she decided to smoke first before heading off to try and catch a bargain or two.

As hoped for, it was two-for-one on Washing Up Liquid. Followed by a bottle of All Surface Kitchen Cleaner and a packet of twenty sponge scourers. Wendy took her time going up and down the aisles looking to spend her money as wisely as possible and soon spotted two-for-one on Chocolate Chip Cookies which she'd always had a soft spot for, but in her current financial situation, dare she treat herself, just this once. Yeah, she dared, because something was most definitely needed to cheer her up and so, they found their way into her basket.

"Right, what's next?" she asks herself, wandering down another aisle. Soon, her eyes couldn't fail to spot a six pack of toilet roll for a pound. Didn't matter in the slightest that it was only two ply, as it was a lot better than what she has had to use lately, as without even thinking twice two packets of them went straight into the basket just as the four tins of meatballs in gravy at fifty pence each. She couldn't care less that they were for children, fifty pence each is fifty pence each, also they would make a nice change from cheap Baked Beans. So, with them, along with two large tins of Vegetable Soup, that was ten pounds accounted for. And when she added one large Shower Gel, one large Toothpaste, two Deodorants and a three-pack of soap. That came to fifteen pounds in total.

Couldn't help but feel a little pleased with herself with what shopping she now had, quite successful and getting the necessities that was required and knowing that there was just that little bit of food now in the cupboard brought a smile to her face. She decided not to pay for her prescription for the painkillers just now as that money may just come in useful for something else and there was Ibuprofen back at the flat in the kitchen cupboard.

McDonald Street Flats may have once been a bright and shining example of modern architecture when they were first built in the late sixties or early seventies, but these days they tell a quite different story. With large chunks of cladding missing and with a permanent dreary appearance, they hardly had a homely feeling about them. But even that couldn't dampen Wendy's positive outlook on life right now, but in approaching the main entrance, she couldn't fail to notice what looked like a man hanging around there. Even though there was still quite a distance between and his face wasn't exactly clearly visible as yet, a strange feeling then came over Wendy, and not in a good way, her gut was for some reason telling her, that this man was looking for her. The closer she got, the more her gut was telling her that, whoever this was, there was something familiar about him.

Without a doubt it looked like this man was waiting for someone as he clearly was making no attempt to enter the building. He just seemed content to stay around the entrance. Wendy had the idea to slow her pace right down as it could be someone looking to collect a debt of her. She wracked her brains for a moment to see if she could think of someone else who wanted money off her. For now, though, no one came to mind. But what, if somehow, a punter had found out where she lived and was hoping to bump into her for a bit of afternoon business as there was still this familiar feeling about him that just wouldn't go away.

Her pace was now at a virtual crawl whilst continuing to look closely at this man who was now standing with his back towards her. Wendy, suddenly, began to get an almost nauseating feeling in her stomach about why this man felt so familiar to her. And her worst fears were then confirmed as he turns around and looks directly at her and a look of surprise completely covers his face when he first claps eyes on her.

"Hello, Wendy, and what the bloody hell happened to you?" David asks.

"Nothing that concerns you," Wendy begins by saying. "What are you doing here and how the bloody hell did you find me?" she then asks, not pleased to see him in the slightest.

"Sharon. You know Sharon? Used to work for you at the florist's. Bumped into her the other night when I was doing some shopping. Told me that you and she were keeping in touch, sending each other the odd message on Facebook. She told me that you lived here in these blocks of flats, but couldn't remember what number. So, what the hell happened to your face then?"

Wendy was seriously unimpressed by all of this. Not just that her friend Sharon had given him a rough idea where she lived, but the fact that he'd actually came around looking for her and she began thinking to herself that it would have been better if it was someone who had come around to cut her off or even a punter.

"Wait until I see her next. She had no right to tell you where I was and what exactly do you want anyway?" I certainly did ask to see you only again," Wendy says feeling not at all happy.

"Look, don't be like this, Wendy. I only came around here hoping that on the off chance that I'd bump into you, and just maybe have a chat, over a cup of tea perhaps."

"Sod off!"

"Oh, come on, Wendy, just one cup of tea. I've been bloody freezing stood out here all this time hoping to see you."

"Well, who's fault is that? You chose to stand out in the cold I'm not making you do it just like I didn't ask to see you." Wendy almost hisses at him.

"Yeah, I know you didn't, I know. But I just wanted to see you. See if you're alright. Maybe you could tell me how I could begin making things up to you which I know I really need to do somehow. There's no getting away from the fact that our marriage failed because of me and I would never say anything different. But it wasn't all bad was it? We did have some good times in the early years didn't we eh?"

No matter how she resented him and what he had done, there was no escaping the fact that what he just said did have some truth about it. The early days were okay, they even had some real fun times.

"Just one cup of tea okay," Wendy firmly tells him. "That's all I want."

"Good, because that's your going to get." Wendy then opens the main entrance using the security code. He offers to carry her bag of groceries.

"Don't need your help thank you."

David wisely backs off and just follows her lead to her flat. Once inside he continues to follow her lead into the kitchen and even though she'd made a concerted effort to clean the entire flat, David still wasn't impressed with it. To him it just looked cheap, but even so, he takes a chair and goes to sit down at the kitchen table.

"Oi! Who said you could sit down?!" Wendy shouts at him.

"Hmmm," was all he could say.

"Exactly, no one said you could sit down, especially not me."

David could now consider himself well and truly told off as he puts the chair back and stands at the table, not even daring to move another muscle for now.

Wendy was more than happy to make him wait before putting the kettle on and taking even more time pouring the water out into the cups once it had boiled.

"Hope you haven't forgotten, no sugar for me because I'm sweet enough," David then says trying a vain attempt at humour hoping to relive the tension that he was clearly feeling from Wendy, who certainly didn't see anything remotely funny in what he just said as the stare that she then gave him clearly indicated.

Once the tea was finally made, the cups were purposely place on opposite sides of the table. Wendy sat down at one end and takes her first sip leaving David stood up wondering what to do next.

"Sit down, you're making the place look untidy," she tells him and very obediently, he did as he was told, remaining at his end of the table as he takes his first sip. Not forgetting to say thank you before doing so.

"So, what exactly brings you around here?" Wendy asks but before he answered that, he had something to ask first.

"Well, firstly, can I ask what happened to your face?"

"No." Was the abundantly clear answer to that question.

"Oh, alright then. It's like I said, bumped into that Sharon and we got talking. Mostly about you and she said that you were living around here somewhere. So, I thought that I'd take a chance and see if I could bump into you and see how you're getting on."

"Well, as you can see, I'm not starving and got a little place all to myself and I'm coping with life without you, so now you've seen haven't you?" Wendy says as point blankly as possible.

"Look, Wendy, I'm not being funny or anything like that, but you can't be doing all that great, I mean look at the state of your face. Are you sure you don't…"?

"No!"

"Oh, okay then, I won't ask again, I promise," he says.

"Good."

"Alright, Wendy, I'm going to level with you now. I came down here looking for you because when I was talking to Sharon, she told me that she'd been hearing things about you."

"Got a lot to say for herself hasn't she," Wendy says with unashamedly sarcasm.

"Well, yeah."

"So, what exactly has she been saying about me then?" I'm dying to know" and despite keeping the sarcastic tone, she was very keen to find out.

"Well, this is just a rumour that she'd heard okay, that's exactly what she said, you know, don't go mad," he begins to tell her.

"Go on."

"To put it bluntly, she said that the rumour was that you're on the game. Is that right?" David asks just as keen to the answer as Wendy was to hear the question. "So?"

"So what?" she asks.

"Is it true?"

"What do you think?"

David paused, took another good look at Wendy's face and at the flat. It may have taken a little while, but he did summon up enough courage to answer her. "I think it's true."

"Oh, do you now. And what makes you think that then, huh?" asks Wendy just as keen to know the answer to his previous question.

"Well, you face for starters because you certainly didn't get any of that by tripping over a kerb or something. Did you? And it's just the way you are right now. You've changed, don't have to be a genius to figure that out. Spotted as soon as I saw you outside. You're hard. I mean really hard. Now, I get that you could be pissed off at seeing me again, but that's not the only reason you're like this right now. You're different and you're are certainly not the gentle, kind, sweet, funny, loving, honest and hard-working girl that I married."

It may have been less than twenty minutes since she set eyes upon him for the first time in god knows how many years, but it was already twenty minutes too long.

"Yeah, you're right, I'm not the gentle or loving girl that you married anymore, and do you know why that is? It's for the same reason that I now live in this crappy little flat and yes, you did hear right from Sharon! I am on the game! I've had to sell myself to just about anyone who at times would have me, just to get by and that's all for the exact reason that my face is the way it is today! And that reason is you! This, the state of my face, this crappy little flat, my life selling myself, is all because of YOU!

"I'm hard now because I've had no choice but to become hard! None! All because of you! Because my name was blacklisted thanks to you. I had to face the Bailiffs because of you. I lost my family defending you. You! Everything that has gone wrong in my life is all down to you! So, don't you dare. Don't you bloody well dare come around here and even think that you can judge me!"

She didn't want to stop there as there was plenty more to get of her chest. Things that have been bottling up inside her for many years just waiting for the day for it all to be unleashed. And this was the day, or so Wendy thought, because what made her suddenly stop was the sight of David doing something that he'd never done before, well, not in front of her anyway, and something that she never thought she'd ever see. Him bursting into tears. Totally and utterly devastated, as his heart was seemingly breaking right now in front of her.

"Wendy, please, I'm so sorry. I honestly and truly didn't come here to judge you. Because I do know that I ruined your life. It was all my fault.

"Look, I'll tell you the truth now. I didn't just come here today to see how you are. I'm here to beg your forgiveness for what I did. And, and I know that you'll probably think that this is mental, but also to beg for another chance."

If was as if Dazza had punched her in the face one more time as Wendy stood there reeling from the shock of what she had just heard. Dumbstruck, utterly dumbstruck, as David somehow managed to pull himself together.

"I know that would probably come as a shock to you but before you say anything else please, please, hear me out."

Wendy didn't have much choice as to hear him out as she was still reeling from what he said to speak for now.

"Wendy, I'm a completely new man now. You're going to find that difficult to believe which I get, but I'm seriously not the same man that you were married to. Got myself all sorted out. My gambling addiction, all gone. Completely gone. Haven't made a bet for well over three years now. Don't even do the lottery and wouldn't even flip a coin these days. I'd just let them win.

"It took a very long time for me to wake up and finally realise what I'd lost after the divorce which, I don't or can't even for a second blame you for wanting, couldn't believe it took so long for the penny to drop. I lost the best thing that had ever happened to me the day the divorce was finally complete. I just didn't see it before, just too wrapped up in myself and my selfish needs.

"Yeah, I know how this is going to sound, promise you I do. But nothing would make me happier if we could try again, to prove to you that I have changed. And that's the truth. Please believe that. Landed a new job, Warehouse Man, decent money plus plenty of overtime. New flat as well, yeah it's council, but it's in a far better area than this one. It's got a decent kitchen with new appliances. I've built my life up again. All that I need now to make it complete, is you.

"Let me make everything up to you. Give you a decent life, one that you really deserve. I can give it to you now. I love you Wendy. You were my first true love, the love of my life. The one I was meant to be with. I'm always going to love you. Please, please, I'm begging you, let me take you away from all of this."

Momentarily, there were no words. Wendy had no words as she stood looking down at him wiping away his tears which, she had to admit, did appear to be genuine enough. But the audacity of him, the downright nerve of him even to think of asking her to, let alone having the brass-neck to actually do it.

"After everything that you put me through!" she began yelling at him. "All the lies, deceit, and just plain embarrassment that I had to suffer because of you. I asked you to get help, remember? In fact, I even begged you at one point and what did you do? Ignore me, didn't you! You just couldn't care less and now you've got the bloody nerve... get out, go on, get out, now!" She meant it, every word. There was no way that Wendy wanted him anywhere near her, especially not right now. And probably never in a million years, despite his protests.

"Wendy, please, let's just talk about it for a minute yeah. We did have some good times to begin with didn't we? You must remember them? We could have then again."

"GET OUT!!"

David looked at her, and even though his eyes were still full of tears, there was also a determination there clearly to be seen.

"I'm not going to give up on you Wendy. I can't give up on you. I'm not going to stop until we're back together. I'll do anything for you and anything to get you back. Please Wendy, at least try again. Give it a trial period if you want."

Wendy then went straight for him but forgetting about her injured ribs as she was soon doubled up in pain. "What's wrong with you Wendy?" A concerned David asks.

"Nothing's wrong! Nothing's wrong, apart from the fact that you're still in my flat and I don't want you to be. Now, if you're not gone in five seconds, I won't be responsible for my actions. Now for the last time, get out!"

"But please, Wendy, can't we just talk?"

"You get this through your thick skull right now! I may be on the game and have to sell myself to get by and yeah, as you can no doubt see, I've been down on my luck for a while, but that doesn't mean that I'll ever consider for one second going back to you, it will never happen. I'd rather stay like this than suffer all the humiliation that you put me through again. Now for the final time, GET OUT!"

David now thought it wise to leave. "Alright, alright, I'll go for now. But I promise you Wendy, I'll be back. I'm not going to give up on you. I love you," were his last words leaving the flat as Wendy slammed the door behind him still fighting the pain in her ribs as she made her way to the living and sat on her sofa.

The anger that he had now made her feel brought a few tears to her eyes as her hands shook which made it very difficult for her to gently hold her ribs in an effort to ease the pain as she cursed David for what he had just asked her. It took an extremely long time for her to settle down but eventually she managed it. From the pocket of her jeans, she takes out her mobile and gets up Martin's number. She just needed to talk to him, that's all. Even if it was just via text message. He did say to call anytime, especially if she needed anything. It wasn't a call to ask for money or food, as all that she needed now was to hear a friendly voice.

She pondered and pondered with her thumb delicately poised over his name and the slightest of touches now, and she'd be dialling him. But she couldn't bring herself to do it. He has a wife and a life to lead and she couldn't expect him to be there all the time. No matter how much she wanted him to be. It just looked like for now, that there would be times when she'd just have to cope by herself.

6

Two weeks later and the taxi driver's sense of relief was becoming more evident to see as now there was one less cackling woman in the back of his cab. He only had two left now and they were only a short trip away, so with any luck, it wouldn't be too much longer before he could have some peace and quiet, and hopefully a decent tip to go along with it before picking his next fare.

"Right, you two take care of yourselves alright, and we'll do this all again soon okay. Bye, bye," says Vanessa to her two friends as the taxi pulls away quite sharply leaving her stood there not really bothering about the cold air as the alcohol that was still clearly in her system from the great night, one which would be remembered for quite some time, kept her warm for now. And now she was safely back home to be near her beloved husband, so there was no reason for her not to be happy right now.

Her happiness grew even more as on entering the kitchen, her husband was waiting already to greet her with a freshly made coffee and a small plate of hot buttered toast.

"Aww, Martin, that for me? That's so lovely it really is, but you didn't have to do that," she says overwhelmed by this gesture.

"Of course, I did," he begins by saying. "You did something very similar for me a few weeks ago, remember?"

"Did I?"

"Yes, you did. When I came home extra late from work one night and you made that cottage pie from scratch for me especially for me. Fresh hot cup of tea as well all waiting for me on the kitchen table when I got back," he reminds her as he could still taste how good it was.

"Oh, Martin, that was different wasn't it eh? You'd been working all hours that week, not just that day. You most certainly earned a treat that week," she says before kissing him on the cheek. "Plus, the mince was due to go off the next day, so it had to be used," she goes on to say with a hint of cheekiness.

"And here's me thinking that you did all that out of the kindness of your heart," Martin says.

"I did, I was being truly kind to you. Couldn't give you out-of-date food and run the risk of you being ill, now could I?"

"Thanks for the kind thought and thinking of my health then," Martin says as they both laugh a gentle laugh together before sitting down at the kitchen table as Martin also had his tea and toast as well. "So, how did the meal go?" he asks.

"Oh, it went really well. Caroline had a lovely time you wouldn't think for a moment that she's fifty-six, now would you? She looks amazing and told us all that her husband, god love him, has booked a weekend away for them both in a country house which they are going to do next weekend. Be nice that, being whisked away for a nice, quiet, romantic weekend somewhere," she says, clearly thinking about it, taking a bite of her toast before saying. "Hint."

"Is it?" asks Martin.

"Yeah."

"As per normal with you, not exactly subtle with it are you?" Martin says to which Vanessa quickly replies.

"Over the years, I've come to learn that subtle hints are usually way above your head," she says again quite cheekily.

"Pushing your luck, you are," Martin tells her.

"Oh really."

"Yes, really."

"So, what are you going to do about it?" she then asks.

"Well, for starters, not going to take you away for a weekend at a country hotel," he tells her.

"Oh Martin, wouldn't it be lovely just to have a short break away somewhere. Doesn't have to be anywhere too expensive, just as long as we can get some quality time together," she says in hope as Martin just looks straight at her.

"Eat your toast," was his pure and simple answer, which Vanessa did, knowing full well that she'd have to work on him a little more if she wanted anything like this out of him just yet.

"I don't know what it is or exactly how you do it, but you always manage to do a lovely piece of toast. Never burnt with always just the right amount of butter on as well. Compliments to the chef," Vanessa says.

"Thanks, nice of you to say, still not taking you anywhere just yet," he says grinning.

"I wasn't going to say anything," Vanessa protested her innocence.

"Yes you were," he then says with that look which clearly suggested that he just knew what she was trying to do and she just looked back at him knowing that she'd have to try again another day while Martin just nodded in acknowledgement of his little victory as he bites into another slice of toast.

"Oh god, I just remembered, there was something that I meant to ask you the other week, I completely forgot about that," she suddenly says.

"The other week?" Martin asks.

"Yeah, well, you know how my mind works sometimes. Well, you should do by now, been married long enough. Anyhow, what it was, I could have sworn that I saw you, Saturday morning I think it was, outside that small supermarket on St Andrew's Avenue. You know, that cheap looking one, can never remember the name of it."

Out of the blue Martin chokes on a piece of toast.

"My God, Martin! You alright?" Vanessa extremely concerned and begins patting him on his back as he coughed and coughed before he reached out and took hold of his cup and somehow managed to take a large drink of his tea which seemed to the trick for now. "You alright now," Vanessa asks still very much concerned for him.

"Yeah... Think so... Must have gone down the wrong hole," Martin says as he coughs a few times more with his eyes watering away.

"You sure? I'm not going to have to do The Heimlich Manoeuvre on you, now am I?" Vanessa somewhat jokingly asks but relived to see him breathing almost normally again.

"No, no you're alright, think whatever it was had gone now," Martin tells her appearing now to be fully recovered.

"Well, that's alright then because it's been years since I done any form of First Aid, probably end up killing you rather than saving you, and we wouldn't want that to happen now would we?"

"No, we wouldn't" Martin wholeheartedly agrees before taking a large mouthful of this tea to ensure that his airway was now all clear.

"So, was it you I saw there then?" Vanessa asks.

"When was this again?"

"About two Saturday's ago. It was that morning that I went to visit Caroline to discuss the arrangements for tonight and I had to get a taxi back as her car was in the garage otherwise she would have happily dropped me back. Could have sworn it was you."

"Two Saturday's ago you say?"

"Yeah."

"That was when I had to deal with that breakdown on the dual carriageway because Rick wasn't feeling too good," he says in his defence.

"Yeah, that's what I thought. Remember you got a text saying about that. But I could have sworn that it wasn't just about seeing you, I'm sure it was the exact same car as well," she says still sure about what she saw that morning.

"The same car as well?" he asks with his eyebrows raised clearly suggesting that maybe she'd better think again.

"Yeah, well, I think so," she says instantly beginning to doubt herself.

"Now, think about this Vanessa. What car have we actually got?" Martin asks confident he already knew that Vanessa would probably get this wrong, yet again.

"Err, right, let's see it's, it's a, Citroen C1. Yes, that's it, a Citroen C1," was her eventual answer and begins looking rather pleased with herself for remembering as Martin begins shaking his head.

"Sorry, wrong again. It's a Toyota Aygo," he informs her.

"Are you sure?" she asks.

"Look out of the window, see for yourself," was Martin's suggestion which Vanessa duly then did and looking very closely at the car.

"Sod it. I always get those two mixed up," as she

sees quite clearly that the word Toyota is written on the boot and not Citroen and being the same shade of red, she saw that morning.

"Don't worry too much about it, it's an easy mistake to make because they are remarkably similar looking cars, just the Peugeot 107 can easily be mixed up with them as well. But it's like I told you, I spent virtually all of that morning on the dual carriage way with that posh couple and their Range Rover."

This was the second time in a space of just a couple of weeks that he had lied to his wife and exactly like the first time he did he truly didn't want to make a habit of doing it, because it was exactly like the previous one, he managed to hide any guilt that he may have been feeling.

"Feel stupid now that after all these years I still can't remember what car we have which, is how many years now?" she asks.

"Four."

"Exactly, four, and it still won't sink into my brain what kind of car we've got," she says but this was soon forgotten as another mouthful of perfectly buttered toast found its way into her mouth as Martin gently laughs as he thought it was quite endearing of her that she still can't remember what car they've got. But also, deep down, quite relieved as well.

"Forget about it for now, it's not as if you're life depends on knowing that or not. Do you fancy a fresh slice of toast?" Martin asks as the dutiful husband.

"Erm, no, yes, no, maybe just one more, it won't hurt, will it?" Vanessa says as it was his pleasure to get up and place one more slice of bread in the toaster and as soon as it was ready, he spread just the right amount of butter onto it and presented it to his wife.

"You spoil me at times you do Martin honestly you do," Vanessa says almost gushing like a teenager looking at her first ever crush as he then joins her. "Aren't you having another slice yourself?"

"No, not just yet. Stick with my tea for now," he says taking another sip before placing it back down on the kitchen table as they both slipped into gazing straight into each other's eyes and both feeling the happiness and the sheer contentment of being with the right person. Martin leaned in for a kiss as Vanessa wondered what took him so long when, totally out-of-the-blue, they both heard a loud 'Ping!'

"Is that my phone or yours," she asks.

"Mine."

"Aren't you going to answer it?"

"Nope."

"Why not?" Vanessa wonders.

"Because I'm going to give you my complete and undivided attention which is also what I'll be doing more of from now on," he says as Vanessa believes he means every word.

"Might be work," she says still very flattered by her husband's previous comment.

"Tough, it's not my night to deal with things. I'm staying right here," he says adamantly.

"Glad to hear that the world of breakdown recovery is going to have to do without you for one night at least, because I need your undivided attention," she tells him seductively as he then goes in for the kiss. But that wasn't going to happen just yet as Vanessa puts a stop to his advances by putting a small piece of toast in his mouth.

"Right, I'm off to bed. You can lock up and I'll see you up there in about five minutes shall we say?" she says smiling away and leaves the kitchen at quite a brisk pace and in no time at all, had literally skipped her way up the stairs to the bedroom.

Forsaking his usual routine of doing all the dishes and packing them away in their appropriate cupboards, he just scrapped what was left on the plates straight into the bin and along with the cups just placed them all in the sink for the morning and begins switching off all the lights on the ground floor before putting the chain across the front door and goes to and stands at the bottom of the stairs. It was then he decides to look at his phone. It was a text message and his heart almost went straight into his mouth, relieved that he didn't answer it in the kitchen as it was message from Wendy. He opens it 'Hello Martin can we talk?"

"You all done down there, Martin?" Vanessa calls down.

"Yeah, all done, just checked that message. You were right it was work, Rick just checking that I'll be at the garage tomorrow morning as we're expecting a few parts to be delivered," he calls back up to her.

"Had a feeling it might be work. You, coming up now?" she calls down.

"On my way," he calls back up to her but before he took one step upwards, he replied to Wendy by saying, 'We will talk soon, I promise,' because there was no way that he was going to ignore her.

7

There was a 'knock, knock, knock' on the door which Wendy really wasn't expecting, especially as it's only just gone nine in the morning, and whilst she's sat at the kitchen table enjoying her small breakfast and savouring every last mouthful of it before lighting up her first cigarette of the day.

'Knock, knock, knock,' again. Whoever this was, didn't sound very friendly, which made Wendy think at first that maybe this was now someone who she owed money to but having had a check through the bills in the drawer under the television, she couldn't remember seeing a final reminder or a threat to be cut off just yet, but she knew that they weren't far away, so it was decided just to carry on with her cigarette wasn't going to face anyone until it had been smoked.

'Knock, knock, knock', even louder this time as Wendy sighs in frustration. "Alright, I'm bloody coming, can't even have a morning fag in peace these days," she says huffing and puffing towards her front door, which when opening, received an unexpected surprise and Wendy could scarcely believe her eyes.

"Well thank god for that, thought there was nobody home for a minute and I hate leaving things like this with neighbours in case they go missing or something and then the arguments start," says a man holding a huge bouquet of flowers and not just any kind of flowers, it was tulips, her favourite. "This is Flat 32, McDonald Street, right?" The man asks.

"Yeah, yeah, that's right," Wendy tells him still with a surprised look.

"Right, here you are you then. Looks like someone loves you then eh," he says, presenting her with the bouquet.

"Love me, I should be lucky," she says seeing the funny side of what he had just told her as then asks, and not wishing to appear rude. "How'd you get through the main door?"

"One of the residents as they were leaving kindly let me in," he says.

"Oh right, well, thanks very much, wasn't expecting anything like this today," she says accepting the flowers before saying goodbye and closing the door and making her way back to the kitchen, "not sure if I've a vase big enough for these. Or any vase at all for that matter," were her next words on entering the kitchen and placing the bouquet which she really liked on the table.

A card was spotted buried deep beneath the tulips and Wendy just had to retrieve and read it to find out who these lovely flowers were from and once the little envelope had been opened, it clearly simply said, 'Hope tulips are still your favourite xxx'.

There was no name on the card to say who it was from, but then again, there didn't need to be, as Wendy now knew exactly who had sent them as the card was immediately then ripped into little pieces and along with the bouquet was thrown straight into the bin. A cigarette was now needed, in order to calm her down as her hands began shaking with temper and it was clear that another cigarette would be needed right after this one.

Once the second cigarette had been smoked and put out, some inner peace had been gained but even so the thought of having a third one now was seriously contemplated and it was only the thought of her current money situation that stopped her, so a fresh cup of tea was called upon instead. It had the desired calming effect that Wendy craved and it was time for her now to get on with her day which began with using the last of her washing powder to wash what was most desperately needed to be washed before heading into the shower.

The bruising on her cheeks were definitely showing signs of going down, so not as much foundation was required today as others previously and the blood-shot eye was almost gone as well but there was still nothing much that she could about her black eye and swollen lip as again, and still for now anyway, it was sensible clothes, trainers and again, she was glad of her Parker Coat because, no sooner had she walked through the main door it wasn't just the cold air that suddenly made her put her fur lined hood up, it was the also the fine and misty rain coming down from the skies as she began walking along the road just as fast as her still injured ribs would allow, in order to keep an arrange appointment. One it appeared that she was looking forward to very much, as her face clearly suggested along with the spring that began to appear in her step.

"Hello Wendy!"

She shrieks out in fright as having no idea who it was that out of nowhere and had sneaked up behind her. And she was even less impressed to turn around to see who it actually was.

"What the bloody hell do you think you're playing

at? Damn near gave me heart attack then!" She shouted as, albeit the best she was able to, took a swing at David who was more than able to move out of the way.

"Sorry Wendy, didn't frighten you, did I? Honestly didn't mean to if I did," he says protesting his innocence.

"What! I mean, what? What the hell do you want David?" she again shouts not caring at all if anyone heard her or not.

"I just, wondered…" he begins.

"What David! What did you wonder, huh? Well come on, what?" Wendy says continuing to shout as David began to feel more than a touch uncomfortable thinking that there might have been people beginning to watch due to Wendy's raised voice. And he was right to think like that as one or two people walking on the other side of the road couldn't help but look back over their shoulders and wonder what all the shouting was about as David took a deep breath before speaking.

"Well, I was wondering whether or not you like the flowers? You still like tulips don't you? They always were your favourite you see, I still remember some things, that can't be bad eh?" he says honestly believing that he had done well. He was immediately soon to find out quite different.

"I don't care if you still remember things or not! What did I tell you yesterday, huh? We're done, over, finished, and we have been ever since the divorce was finalised, okay! I don't want to see you anymore! In fact, it wouldn't bother me in the slightest if I never saw you again! Now, just leave me alone will you!"

David was stunned into silence after hearing all of this, even more so when Wendy actually tried to physically push him away, the pain in her ribs dictated that not very successfully as she hardly budged him as it appeared that he couldn't or maybe even stubbornly refused understand her point of view.

"What, you don't like tulips anymore? Fine, I'll get you some others, just tell me what you want."

"It's not just about the flowers you idiot! Don't you get it? I'm not interested in you anymore. I don't want anything to do with you and I certainly do not want you anywhere in my life. Now, is there any part of that you didn't get because I'll happily repeat it for you!" Wendy says still screaming at him.

"And when I told you that I wasn't going to give up on you, what part of that did you not get?" He tells her, not just with sincerity, but also with a clear determination as he had now raised his voice without a single care who heard him. As one woman who was walking her dog clearly did as she just had to look back over her shoulder at them as Wendy tries to push him away, but, yet again, without much success.

"Just go will you, just go, and give up on me," she says.

"I can't Wendy, I love you," he tells her ad no matter how he believed that he meant these words, Wendy, was still having none of it.

"Well I don't love you, alright! I stopped loving you a long time ago after what you did to me. Now, just get lost and leave me alone, got it!"

Wendy then just storms off leaving David stood there utterly speechless as she wasn't just angry about what he had done with the flowers, nor the fact that he'd scared her half to death, but she was now angry at the fact that he had put her in a bad mood which was the last thing that she wanted to feel like with her appointment not too far away.

Martin then thought to himself, that if he headed for that Tesco's Metro he used a few weeks ago, for the teabags and Victoria Sponge, then he'd be able to take his bearings from there and take the first left back into Ivydale Street where The Sailors Arms was.

So, that's exactly what he did, because after a few more minutes driving, he suddenly spotted the Tesco's, then all he had to do was take the first left and there he was, relived at not getting lost and driving past The Sailors Arms where he now parked not too far away from.

A glance at his mobile told him that he still had a few minutes to spare, so he used this time to prepare himself. Firstly, physical. Well, he was still working, and this was his lunch hour so, his overalls were as clean as they could possibly be as thankfully he hadn't had any major jobs this morning that would have covered him in oil or grease. And combine that with a white T-shirt, which was still actually white, then he wasn't looking too bad, considering that the person that he was meeting would understand that this is a working day for him.

As for mentally prepared, totally different kettle of fish that one. As he had to keep reminding himself that this was just a friendly lunchtime drink and chat nothing more, nothing less. Especially nothing more as he had a lovely wife at home, so there was certainly not going to be nothing more involved in this. Yet he still couldn't help but feel nervous. Just like being a love-sick teenager oh his very first date all those years ago.

Apart from bumping into Wendy a few weeks ago, he didn't know this area very well, he only knew that it had an unsavoury reputation which showed even more now in the daylight as he got the clear sense that strangers weren't exactly made to feel welcome around here as he double checks that he's locked his pick-up lorry before heading into the unknown, otherwise known as The Sailors Arms.

His first impression on entering, hated it, didn't like it one little bit, and not many could blame him as it hardly gave out a welcoming feeling, as the handful of customers who were already there, all clapped their unfriendly eyes on him and from that very moment, he felt liked a marked man. Martin's initial thought was to get out quick while he was still able to, but he couldn't. He was meeting someone and the last thing that he wanted to do, was to let that person down.

He bravely fully entered and walked straight up to the bar conscious not to make eye contact with any of the customers who purposely followed his every move. He was clearly having difficulty with the sticky carpet and the less he saw of the brown and dirty mustard yellow colour scheme the better and the ripped upholstery on the majority of the seats and stools hardly made sitting a comfortable option. And as for being called The Sailors Arms, well, the only nautical thing within it was a rather old looking Sailors Knot board, mounted on a wall tucked away in the corner.

On making his final approach to the bar, he kept his focus solely in front of him and nowhere else, especially not to his right where a scruffy grey-haired man wearing a military camouflage combat jacket and tattered jeans who was hugging a pint of Guinness sat at the bar and kept staring at Martin with a mean look in his eye and it was quite clear that one wrong word, even spoken accidentally, could set this man off and as Martin had never been much of a fighter, he just decided just to let this man look and not say anything until he finally reaches the bar.

"Pint of Diet Coke please?" Martin asks meekly but still politely as the barmaid and the man at the bar both now look at him wondering what sort of man he actually was ordering something like that in a place such as this where the more illegal deals there are, the better the regulars like it.

"Coke?" the barmaid asks somewhat disbelievingly giving Martin the impression that he had to justify his order very quickly.

"Humm, yeah, got to go back in an hour plus I'm driving," he says. The barmaid just shrugs her shoulders as if to say, 'fair enough' and began pouring his drink and he could see that there were some hot snacks available in the glass case at the end of the bar. "Alright if I have a Steak and Kidney Pie as well please?"

"Only got Chicken and Mushroom left," the barmaid was quick to answer.

"Oh, alright then. Tell you what I'll take two of them please and two sausage rolls as well if that's alright," he asks deciding that the more polite he is, the less likelihood of anyone wanting to pick a fight with him as his focus still remained very much in front of him. So, much so in fact, he was completely oblivious to a woman who was now coming out of the ladies and showing no decorum wiping her hands dry in her denim jacket who had now spotted Martin and was thinking to herself that it just might be worth a try as she brazenly walks straight up to him and puts her arm around his waist.

"Hello there handsome, how are you? Looks like you're in the chair, so how about buying me a drink and letting me keep you company for a bit and see if we get on. I reckon we just might y'know. Got a good feeling about you."

Being caught completely unaware , Martin almost jumps out-of-his-skin and then turns to his left to see at least a size eighteen woman stood there grinning away at him before trying be seductive as she possible could, flicking her long, curly, jet black wet look hair as underneath her jacket was black top which, just like Tanya's bra, struggled to contain her over-inflated chest and as he took a quick glance down, the black leggings that she was wearing not only needed washing, but done her powerlifting thighs no favours whatsoever.

"Thanks, that's kind of you to offer, but I'm actually meeting someone here. She should be here anytime now," he tells her again being polite as he possibly could.

"Well, she's not here, now is she? So, why not let me keep you company until she does. Just a Vodka and Coke. Single will do because I'm a cheap night out, if you catch my drift," she says with a wink and a cheeky grin as Martin was thinking that cheap was exactly the right word for her as he again, politely as possible, declines her offer.

"Your bloody loss then," she snorts somewhat in disgust and clearly a touch offended at being turned down before walking away as she then spots another man who was sat quite close the Knot Board all by himself with his half-finished pint of lager and she wastes no time at all in approaching him and he clearly seemed to be more receptive towards her and was more than happy to buy her the Vodka and Coke that she wanted which Martin was relieved to see as it would mean, that for now at least, she'd be leaving him alone.

If it wasn't for the fact that he was meeting someone, Martin could have happily walked out of this dive as he thought it to be and never set foot in here again as his order then arrives and whilst he was busy paying for it, he didn't notice that the main door had opened and within a short minute, Wendy was tapping on his shoulder. He turns around, extremely pleased to see her.

"Oh, hello there, you okay? You could say that is perfect timing on your part. What would you like to drink with your food?" he asks smiling.

"Food?" Wendy asks miffed.

"Yeah, it's not much, just a chicken and mushroom pie and a sausage roll, as I was going to have something anyway, so I thought that I won't be rude and eat in front of you, so got you something as well."

"Oh, right, thanks, that's nice of you," she says.

"No problem, drink?"

"Err, yeah, okay, if that's really okay with you, could I have a Gin and Tonic please?" she asks somewhat reluctantly not really wishing to abuse Martin's generosity as he turns right back to the barmaid.

"Make that a double for her, if that's okay?" The Barmaid was only too happy to oblige as there was soon a double Gin and Tonic along with everything else which they shared carrying to the nearest available table.

"Thanks for this, Martin. Can't deny was feeling a little peckish," Wendy says tucking straight into the pie.

"Hey, it's no problem. Like I said, I was going to have something myself so you'd just as well eat as well. So, how have you been keeping?" Martin asks seeing that her blood-shot had begun to ease off, and guessing that there was enough foundation on her face to cover the bruising on her cheeks but, unfortunately for her, her black eye and swollen lip remained clearly visible.

"I'm okay, I suppose, getting by as they say. Martin, look, I'm sorry that I contacted you again the other day. I know that I can't keep relying on you. It was just, I was in a bit of a low place, hoping to hear a friendly voice I suppose but I mean it, you'll hardly hear from me from now on, except when I'm going to pay you back and I promise you Martin, I will one day and that's the God honest truth."

"Oi you, less of that alright," Martin leapt in to say. "Told you before, you contact me anytime you want alright and I'll always get back to you just as soon as I can. Just sorry it took a little while to reply to your text, was a bit busy at the time, anyway, here you are," he says slipping her some money underneath the table.

"Sorry it's only fifty for now but if you do need anymore don't hesitate to ask and I'll see what I can do for you okay... What's the matter Wendy? You look as though you're about to burst into tears, hey, calm down."

He wasn't far wrong as Wendy was indeed beginning to fill up with tears. But it was tears of gratitude that were coming.

"Take no notice of me, Martin, just being a daft old cow. I'm so grateful to you Martin, honestly, if I'd hadn't spotted you down here a couple of weeks ago and jumped into your car, really don't know where I'd be right now. I was truly at my wits end, seriously I was. So, if it looks as if I'm going to burst into tears, it's because that I'm so grateful to you," she says finally forcing a smile hoping that it would stop any tears from falling which, for now, did appear to work.

"You don't have to keep thanking me, Wendy, honestly you don't. Always going to be here for you," he tells her.

"Yes, I do have to keep thanking you, Martin, if for no other reason than you have a wife and a home which I'm sure that the money that you've lent to me is taking a fair chunk out of the housekeeping. Have you said anything about this to your wife yet?" Wendy asks.

"No, not a word," Martin answered immediately.

"Martin, you should y'know. She has every right to know. Especially as we're not doing anything wrong really. You're just helping out a friend."

"I know that we're not doing anything wrong Wendy," he begins looking at her thinking at the same time 'More's the Pity'. But it's like I told you before, what goes on with my marriage and what goes on with you are two entirely different things. To be kept apart and in no way to interfere with each other, alright." Martin certainly had now spoken on this subject and Wendy decided that it was best not to argue with him and changes the subject very quickly.

"How's work going then?"

"Yeah, not too bad," he says.

"Hoping to be back full-time myself soon, wonder if anyone has missed me," she once again couldn't resist finding the humour of her recent run of bad luck but once again, Martin didn't see the funny side, but was beginning to understand why she now, says such things. But that doesn't mean that he had to like them, which Wendy couldn't fail to notice.

"Sorry Martin, shouldn't have said that. I know that you don't get my sense of humour when it comes to this," she says apologetically.

"No, no, you don't you dare be sorry, like you

rightly said before, I've got no right to judge you. I just wish," Martin stops dead of what he was going to say next, clearly struggling with what he wanted to say next.

"Wish what, Martin?" That I didn't have to do it?" Wendy asks him.

"Can still read me like a book then I see," begins Martin as Wendy tips him a wink. "Yeah, you're right. I really wish that you didn't have to do any of this. Wish that I could more for you."

"Hey, you, you've done more than enough, honestly you have, so don't go thinking anything different okay," she tells him reaching out her hand to take hold of his which just felt so natural to do.

"Okay, if you say so, but don't you go worrying about paying me back until you're actually able to, alright," he tells her reaching out his other hand to take hold of her other hand which again, just felt so natural to do and even more naturally, was to begin gazing into each other's eyes and accidentally slipped into looking something like Puppy Love.

"Aww, don't you two make a lovely couple," the barmaid says from behind the bar. Both Martin and Wendy instantly let go of each other's hands and if the barmaid hoped to cause these two some embarrassment, then it was mission accomplished which she the pleasure she gained from it was clear for all the world to see.

"Right, I best get back to work," Martin says suddenly realising what the time was.

"Oh, right, so you have," Wendy then says as they both wolfed down the last of their lunches as Martin, who was more than happy to see Wendy again, felt a lot better when he was outside.

"Do you want a lift anywhere? I've still got few minutes to spare," he says.

"Nah, honestly I'll be okay," Wendy politely declines.

"But it's still raining," he was quick to point out.

"It's only that fine misty stuff, and I've got my big coat, I'll be alright," she says before, and catching Martin completely unawares, throwing her arms around him. "Thank you so much again Martin and not just for the money. Thanks for being there for me, that's the most important thing." Martin, still thinking that her ribs may just still be sore and tender then ever so gently, put his arms around her.

"Hey you, always going to be for you okay, you know that," he says as they just hold each other with neither one in a great hurry to let the other go especially as a tear then came from Wendy's better eye which she absolutely did not want Martin to see and as quickly and discreetly as possible, wiped it away before finally letting him go.

"Don't forget, Wendy, you contact me anytime okay," he says truly meaning it.

"Alright, Martin and thank you, but I'll always text you first okay, bye for now," and with planting the best possibly kiss, that her swollen lip would allow, onto his cheek and clearly it was a struggle for her to walk away. But walk away she did, which thankfully for her she did move as a blur appeared out of nowhere and the next thing either one of them knew, Martin was on the floor as David, in a jealous rage began pounding on him in the hope of causing serious injury as he yells. "STAY AWAY FROM MY WIFE!!"

Martin was defenceless and David relentlessly kept hitting him. Wendy screamed for someone to help, but this being Ivydale Street, fights were not only commonplace, but often encouraged as the one or two who were stood around didn't batter an eyelid. Wendy now knew that it was going to up to her alone to do something as summoning up all the strength that she could, walked up behind a kneeling David, and with what claws she had, reached over and dig them as hard as she could into his forehead causing not only to scream himself, but also to stop hitting Martin as he stood up under her control before she manages to push him away. He turns to look at her which he instantly regrets as he'd never been slapped so hard before by anyone which sent him reeling backwards.

"Just what do you think you're doing? I'M NOT YOUR WIFE ANYMORE!! What I do or who I see is none of your business! You finally got that! No get out of here before I kill you myself! GET OUT OF HERE, NOW!" Wendy's rage now knew no bound towards David now, and he finally knew it as he wanted to speak to defend his actions, thinking that he was in some way protecting her, maybe even offer an apology of some sort, but he just knew it would be a futile gesture. He had gone too far. He knew it. As Wendy then knelt down over Martin, practically in tears to see if he was alright, David knew that it would be best for him to leave as the woman who he believes he still dearly loves, clearly cared for someone else.

8

It may now be coming to the end of the first week of December and the weather was certainly now growing increasingly colder by the day, but David wasn't paying too much attention to the weather, he had just thrown himself into his work. If there were any extra hours to be had, he was the first to volunteer for them. If it meant doing a double shift, he was the man to do it as he just needed to keep himself, and his mind occupied, the last thing that he needed to do now was to sit around, being lonely, as that would give him the chance to dwell on recent events. He just couldn't handle that.

He wandered around the warehouse looking for something to do, anything would have done. Didn't matter that he'd already been there for twelve hours today, he just didn't want to stop just yet. Walking down one aisle, he spots old Albert, who was clearly struggling to lift a box, and David just couldn't bear to see this so, without hesitation, he goes right up to him and put the box onto the first shelf exactly where Albert asks him to put it.

"Albert, don't you ever struggle like that again okay. If you ever need any help you just come and find me alright. Can't have you doing yourself a nasty injury can we eh?" David tells him as Albert then not only thanks him for his kind assistance, and promises that in future, he'll seek his help as suddenly they here a man call out.

"Oi, David!"

They both turn around to see the boss, Tim Willis, was now pointing directly at him.

"Yeah boss," David answered.

"Quick word in the office before you leave tonight okay mate," Tim said before turning away and heading straight back into his office and closing the door behind him.

"You in any trouble, David?" Albert asks hoping that he wasn't.

"Not that I know of Albert, mate. Wonder what he wants?" David says curious to know before saying to Albert. "Right mate, I'll see you next week alright, take it easy and have a good weekend alright."

Albert says thanks again and goodbye as David

heads towards the boss's office still wondering what it was all about.

*

Both the black eye and swollen lip had recovered sufficiently enough now, before attempting now to touch her toes and do some other stretches, which although there were still twinges of pain, Wendy knew that it was time to go back to work and was soon sat in front of her bedroom mirror applying the right amount of make up to cover up what remained of her injuries to make herself at least, look respectable, With one final, but still gentle, touch of lipstick, it was now time to get dressed and already knowing that it was going to be a cold night, there was a pair of tight black leather trousers hanging up in her wardrobe ready to be worn.

*

"Knock, knock, alright if I come in, Tim?" David asks holding the door slightly ajar.

"Yes, of course, come on in, David," Tim was happy to cordially invite him in. "Look, I know it's Friday and you've almost finished for the day, so I won't keep you too long. Shut the door behind you," Tim says and judging by his calm and relaxed tone of voice, David had no need to be worried as doing as Tim says he shut the door behind him and walked up to his desk.

"Right, David, I'll get straight to the point. There's a supervisor vacancy come up. After that heart attack he had and thank the lord he's out of danger now, Freddie has now decided to take early retirement. Which is probably the best thing that he could do but, that still leaves me having to fill his job, and I thought that you might be interested."

Even though he had been hoping for some recognition for all his work and service to the company, this still came as quite a surprise to him.

"Who me?" David asks.

"Yes David, you. And why not you, huh? You've certainly put in enough work and effort around here, especially these last couple of weeks, you've been like a man possessed. It's no secret that you can do the job, probably standing on your head more than likely, but most of all, I'm quite sure that the lads will listen to you. They'll respect you David because you've worked you're way up. Look, to being with it will be only temporary, and it will mean working nights for now, but if all goes well for let's say, three months, the job will be yours and as soon as the opportunity comes up, if you want, we'll put you back on the day shift if you want to, alright? What do you say?" David looked so overwhelmed that he hardly knew what to say for now, it took him a minute or two for him to burst out with.

"Yeah, of course I'll take it Tim. Thank you so much and I promise that I won't let you down honestly I won't."

"Take it your pleased then, David?" Tim asks smiling and sharing his joy.

"Pleased. Of course, I'm pleased and trust me, you've chosen the right man for the job," David not just assures him but promises him.

"Yeah, I know that I have," Tim begins. "Right, start Monday night, okay."

"Yeah okay."

"Right, now get yourself out and have a great weekend, you've earned it, see you here Monday night," Tim tells him and David didn't need telling twice as grabbing his coat from the changing rooms, he leaves with an almighty spring in his step just as Wendy, now all fully dressed, as once again had to step out into a world that she hated and so dearly wished that she didn't have to do.

*

Once Wendy, had arrived at Ivydale Street, she knew only too well that she had to be extra vigilant as there was no way she wanted a repeat of the incident that happened here a couple of week ago. The plan was to duck into an alleyway which was directly opposite The Sailors Arms where there was some noise coming out from, but not much to suggest that it was doing a roaring trade tonight, where she could stay in the shadows and just keep her eye on the street for any potential business.

The night air was getting colder and colder by the minute as she huddled against the wall in an effort to try and keep herself warm, ensuring that her jacket remained fully zipped up looking up and down what was for now an empty street and thinking how nice it would be now if some nice man came along with a nice warm car but more importantly, willing to spend plenty of his money for her company.

No sooner had she wished this then, as if by magic, from the far end a car turned right and into the street which Wendy spotted in a flash.

"Aye, aye, this could be someone now," she says watching it come slowly towards her seemingly in no rush to leave the street. Wendy's gut, as well as doing this sort of work for quite some time now, was telling her that she could be in luck here. "Right, let's see what happens here," she says slowly but surely emerging from the shadows but still keeping an ever watchful eye-out for any of the other girls, especially Tanya, and once satisfied it was safe, he pace quickened up and headed straight towards the car who had clearly noticed her and slowly pulled up at the kerb alongside Wendy as the electric window was lowered.

"Hello there my love you, aright there? Is there anything that I can do for you?" Wendy asks the best charming smile that she was physically able to.

The man behind the steering wheel had a scarf covering the bottom part of his face and also wearing a baseball cap which only left his eyes exposed and he seemed to be making a point of not looking directly at Wendy.

"Yeah, hiya love, look, I'm just looking for a bit of company for an hour or so. Nothing word or kinky, just someone to spend some time with. Maybe get a something to eat if you fancy doing that?" Were the muffled words that Wendy heard coming through the scarf.

"Is that all you want?" Wendy asks.

"Yeah, honestly that's it. Just come for a drive with me," the man says still sounding muffled as Wendy decided that it was time to get down to business.

"Alright then, how much are you willing to spend?"

"I got a hundred in cash for your time, plus obviously I'm buying the food of you want to. What do you say?" The man asks still not looking directly at her. The mere fact that this man refused to look at her whilst still with most of his face covered, in which was no doubt quite a warm car may have aroused some suspicions in most people.

"You're on," she says without any thought to any potential danger as the lure of a warm car, some much needed money, and a bite to eat was far too much for her to say no to as she jumps in, puts on her seat belt as they pull away. Past, The Sailors Arms, and turned right.

"If you're really thinking of getting something to eat, there's a half decent Burger and Kebab place not too far from here and I must admit a Cheeseburger, with a splash of tomato sauce, few fried onions, you could even make it a double if you're feeling a bit flush. So, what's your name?" Wendy asks feeling quite chatty.

The man didn't say anything for now, especially now as they were heading into the main part of town with all the bright lights from the shops, pubs, streetlights, that now completely surrounding them as he seem to pre-occupied with still not looking at Wendy who couldn't help but look at the man's eyes as suddenly, she had a horrible feeling in the pit of her stomach that his eyes were strangely familiar to her. In a flash, she reaches over and pulls down the man's scarf and here worse fears were now confirmed. "How dare you!"

"Hello, Wendy," David says.

"You just stop this car right now and let me out alright! This is kidnapping of some sort I'm sure it is," Wendy says angrily.

"How can it be kidnapping when you got into the car willingly, huh?" David begins by asking to which Wendy, for now, had no answer. "Look, I'll buy you a Cheeseburger if you're hungry, I'll even make it a double of you want, with tomato sauce and fried onions. I'll even give you the hundred pounds I promised I'd pay just please, please, let me show you something that's all I ask. Promise I won't take up much of your time honestly, I won't. It's important that you see this," he says.

"Why would I want to see anything that you've got to show me, huh? After what you did the other day to my friend!!"

"I know, I know, I shouldn't have done that," David begins remorsefully. "Have you spoken to him lately, how is he?"

"You don't get to ask how he is okay, so don't you dare try and act all sorry with me alright! All you need to know is that he'll always be twice the man that you'll ever be. Now pull over and let me out, now!"

Wendy demanded.

"I know I was wrong and I'm sure what you just said is right, but Wendy please I have to show you something," David begins to plead with her.

"Let me out, David, I mean it!"

"No."

"David, I'm not joking with you. Let me out!"

"Wendy, just one chance, that's all I'm asking. Please?"

"Right, that does it," Wendy says and without a single ounce of fear, she places one hand on the steering wheel and turns it towards the pavement.

"What are you doing!" David shouts as he fights her off to regain control, but Wendy wasn't done, not by a long way and makes another grab for the steering wheel but David was anticipating this and held up his left in attempt to stop her but Wendy just didn't know when to stop as well as attempting to get to the steering wheel whilst screaming and shouting obscenities causing the car to serve which many people walking along the brightly lit streets couldn't fail to notice as thankfully, there was hardly any traffic on the roads, a set of traffic lights then appeared which were on red as David slammed on the brakes.

"Right, that's enough, you've could have gotten both killed!" David yells in her face causing Wendy to move back but still with her rage clearly showing. "All I want to do is show you something alright! If don't like it, then fine, you go, alright, but just let me show you okay. I'll still pay the hundred pounds and even buy you a Double Cheeseburger if you're that hungry."

"Don't want your money or you're food!" Wendy shouts.

"Alright, don't have them then, but you're coming with now, got that!" David wasn't too be argued with now, Wendy knew that look in his eye, so she just sat back in her seat, and complied. She still didn't like it, but she complied thinking to herself that the sooner this was other and done with, the sooner she would be rid of him as the lights then turn green and they pull away. And after a few minutes of driving in silence, David parks up, and if Wendy wasn't happy about all of this before, she most certainly is now.

"Right, what the hell are we doing here?" Wendy asks not at all pleased, whilst looking at an Amusement Arcade.

"Wendy, please trust me on this one," David says as he takes hold of her hand to reassure her, but Wendy was having none of it.

"Five seconds to tell me what's going on, or I'm off," she says clearly in mood for any of his games.

"I can't tell you Wendy, I have to show you.

Please, trust me, just this one time." David literally pleaded with her for this one chance which he knew only full well, would probably the only one that he would get as Wendy looked at him, still not really trusting him fully.

"Alright, alright, David, let's get this over and done with," she says getting out of the car as fast as humanly possible while David followed suit as he wanted to lead her in.

Once inside, Wendy was not in the least impressed by her surroundings as this is the last place that she'd ever thought she would find herself again as David, still leading her, was totally focused on heading for particular area, which she knew only full well where that was. David had never had much of an interest in computer or video games. The thought of killing aliens on a faraway planet to secure the freedom of the galaxy, or racing around the streets of Monaco at night in order to become World Champion never really entered his mind. He had another area in which he wanted to get to which was going to bring back horrible memories for Wendy. Like the rent not being paid amongst other bills, so when they entered the area which had the sign 'No Under 18's Allowed Past This Point' Wendy just wanted to leave straight away.

The flashing lights on the Fruit Machines and the

noises they made and the promises of huge jackpots, once turned David into an overgrown child and he just had to play them until he won something. Didn't have to be the jackpot, just anything, even if it was only two or three pounds after spending about ten or twenty as they both in the very middle of all these machines.

"Right, what the hell are you playing at David? You know how much I hate these machines just like any form of gambling. Is this some kind of joke? Well, is it? Wendy wanted answers, and she wanted them now."

"Alright, I know how bad this looks, Wendy, but honestly, I've brought you here for a very good reason. Take a good look at where we are," he says.

"Yeah, I know exactly where we are, thank you very much don't need you to remind me. I should smack you in the mouth right now," and Wendy's temper was a clear indication that she was more than happy to do exactly that.

"Yeah, and normally I wouldn't disagree with you and I would deserve it but look around again at where we are but more importantly, look at me. Please?" David asks. Wendy didn't understand why he would want her to look at him, so he decided to use a different tactic.

"Think about it, Wendy," David begins, "five, six

years ago, could I stand here right now and not put any money in any one these and start playing? We both know the answer is no. Even if it meant looking for any spare loose change to stick into one of these things. Didn't matter which one, just as long as I was playing, gambling, being utterly selfish. Wouldn't have given you a second thought, would I eh? You could have been sat at home worrying yourself sick about food and all the bills that were mounting up around our ears.

"But look at me now Wendy. Not even itching to play any of one of them. I can stay here all night and not even think for one second to put any money into one of these bloody things. I don't need them anymore, not like I did in the past when I was addicted. But I'm a reformed character now. A totally changed man.

"Had some good news today at work, I'm going to be promoted to Night Shift Supervisor. It might be only three-month trial period, but the boss said if I do well, he'd offer me the job permanently.

"I've finally got myself sorted out and my life back on track Wendy. I know it took a while and I'll never forget what I did to you. All the embarrassment and shame that you went through because of me and that'll be something I'll probably never be able to make up for properly. But I'd like to try. Please Wendy, at least let me try and make things up with you. I can now give you a good life because as you can see for yourself, I'm cured, I'm no longer an addict. And it's not just in here, bookies, casinos, never go near them. I can now devote myself to the woman that I love. And that's you Wendy, it's always been you."

He drops to his knees in one last desperate attempt to win back the woman who he truly loves and Wendy had never seen or heard such an honest, and also heartfelt plea in all her life and no matter how much she wanted to, she just didn't have the heart to tear him to shreds again. She helps him to his feet and gently put her arms around him and begins to whisper.

"You did, David, you beat your addiction, I believe you did it you truly did and I'm so, so proud of for doing that. But the truth is, and I can't lie to you, I just don't love you anymore. I believe you when you say that you'll do anything for me, and that's so wonderful to hear, but if I can't do the same for you then it's just not going to work, I wouldn't be treating you fairly.

"Please see, David, that if you carry on with chasing me, you'll just tear us apart and neither of us want that do we? No, we don't. You're free, David, free of that addiction, so you can live your life now, move forward, and be happy."

She couldn't leave him without planting a gentle kiss on his cheek and hoping that he would give her one last hug. Which he very reluctantly did as he watched her walk out of his life for good, knowing that, no matter how much he was hurting right now, it was the best thing for both of them.

A couple of hours later, Martin stepped out of the shower feeling all clean and invigorated and all set for a cosy night in with his wife as she hears that he's out of the bathroom. "Martin!" she calls up.

"Yeah."

"Hope you don't mind, because I know that I don't normally do it. But while you were in the shower, you phone went off, I only answered because I thought it might be work or an emergency," she explains.

"Oh, okay, don't worry about it. Was it anything serious?" he shouts down.

"To do with work it was. It was some woman called Wendy," Martin stopped dead in his tracks on the top landing when he heard this, relieved that Vanessa couldn't see the look of horror which was now clearly across his face as the very moment he heard the name Wendy, he knew exactly which

Wendy it was.

"Oh really," he answers trying to remain calm so as not to give anything away.

"Yeah, she said something like she just needs one more part for her Fiesta and then everything's sorted out. Said you knew what she meant by that. Is that right?" she asks from the bottom of the stairs. Martin, by now, was in the bedroom with the door slightly ajar, horrified that Wendy had actually phoned before sending a text first like she always said she would.

He was suddenly a bag of nerves and cursing the fact that he'd left his mobile unattended so that Vanessa could get to it. That'll have to change from now on, he won't let it out of his sight.

"Hurry up, Martin, your tea's getting cold!" Vanessa calls up to him.

"Coming!" he calls down from the bedroom, putting on his dressing gown before taking a deep breath and hoping that he has done enough to compose himself before going down the stairs.

9

Monday morning had come around again and just like so many others, it was back to work for Vanessa, but to say that her mind wasn't exactly on the job in hand, was a touch of an understatement. It looked as though she was not giving her full and undivided attention to the couple, who looked about to be both in their mid-thirties, who were sat on the other side of her desk telling her exactly what they were looking for.

"Right, let's see what we can find shall we? So, it's two weeks, self-catering in Malta any time after Mid-August. Hopefully, that shouldn't be too difficult to find something for you both," Vanessa says clearly not registering what she had just been told as they first looked at each other before turning back to Vanessa.

"Err, no," the man begins. "We wanted ten days, full or half-board in Cyprus for the beginning of July next year." He finishes as they both look at her hoping this time, she's understood what they wanted this time.

"Oh, of course, oh my god I'm so sorry. Of course, what on earth was I thinking of. I'm just not quite with it this morning. Had a bit of a long weekend I'll spare you all the details but I've come into work today for a break. Right, let's try again shall we. So, it's ten days, full or half-board, in Turkey…"

"Cyprus," the man interrupts to remind her.

"Yes, yes, of course Cyprus of course, sorry, and it was for September…"

"July, next year," the woman then jumped in to remind her.

"Yes, yes of course July," Vanessa says still not inspiring a lot of confidence to the couple that she knew what she was doing as Caroline comes up from behind her with a friendly tap on her shoulder.

"Really sorry to interrupt you all," she begins before turning directly to the couple and asks. "How are you two this morning, all alright?" Before leaning down and whispering in Vanessa's ear. "Ritchie, Area Manager Ritchie that is, has arrived and wants to see you in Rebecca's office. In private." It was something that Vanessa clearly was not expecting to hear.

"What, me?" she asks.

"Yes, you," Caroline says before telling her. "Don't worry, I'll take over here," she kindly offers.

"Oh, okay then, this is Liz and Terry, and they're looking to go to, go to… Cyprus next July, right?" Vanessa says hoping upon hopes that she finally got it right, which of course she had but both Liz and Terry, although on the outside were pleased that she had finally got it right, but on the inside, both were glad that Caroline was taking over in case Vanessa made any mistakes on the actual booking as she left them to it and made her way to Rebecca's office.

When she gets to the door, she stops and waits nervously before doing anything and thinking to herself that there was no reason to be here for doing anything wrong as such. In fact, the more that she thought about it, the more convinced of that she was which begs the question, why the Area Manager wanted to see her. In private. Being uncertain of anything had always made her a touch nervous which was why it was only a timid knock on the door that she then gave and instantly wondered if it was loud enough for anyone to hear.

"Come in." Obviously, it was as Vanessa takes a deep breath and enters to see Ritchie sat behind the desk with a warm and welcoming smile.

"Hi Vanessa, and there's no need to look so

scared, nothing to be frightened of I'm not going to eat you or anything. Come on in and take a seat," he says waving her in which made Vanessa immediately begin to feel a lot more at ease, which seemed to be a knack that her younger area manager had of doing, which always impressed her, in the same way that he had risen in such a short space of time (only just over five years) to achieve what he has but always remained level-headed, and respectful to everyone. Vanessa does as he says and takes a seat. Now managing a smile. "How are you Vanessa? It's been a while since I've saw you last," he says.

"I'm okay thanks, and yes, it has been a while since we last saw each other. Wasn't it at Rebecca's barbecue back in June?" she says.

"Christ, yeah it was, I remember it now. Good day it was as well. Apart from when Rebecca's son had too much ice cream," he says.

"Oh yeah, he did, didn't he? It was like something out of *The Exorcist* wasn't it? Poor lad," Vanessa says.

"Poor mummy and daddy, having to clean it all up," Ritchie then says as they both cringe at the thought of it before he goes on to ask. "And how's your husband, Martin isn't it? What is it he does for a living again, mechanic is it?"

"Yeah, mechanic, but he also does Breakdown

Recovery as well. Yeah, he's fine thanks for asking," she tells him.

"That's good to hear. Right, suppose you're wondering why it is I've asked to see you?" says Ritchie as Vanessa couldn't help but begin to wonder again.

"Well, yeah."

"Again, there's no need to be frightened, it's a good thing that you're here. Well I think so anyway. As you're probably aware, Rebecca is soon to be leaving us, which reminds me, must buy her a coffee to say thanks for her letting me use her office. Can't deny I was disappointed when she told me, but, if she feels that her future lies elsewhere, well, best of luck to her. But that does mean of course, there's a manager's vacancy going here," he says looking directly at Vanessa who suddenly realises what he's implying.

"Me?" she asks surprised.

"Yes, Vanessa, you," Ritchie tells her with no nonsense about it.

"Oh my god, Ritchie, why on earth made you think of me? I mean if you'd seen me out there less than ten minutes ago. I was with a couple out there and I couldn't even remember when or even where they wanted to go. Honestly, you wouldn't have trusted me to put the kettle on, never mind run this place. I take it, it is this branch that you were referring to?"

"Yes, it is."

"Gosh, I didn't see this coming at all which you've probably noticed," she says smiling not really knowing what else to say for now.

"Why you?" Ritchie begins by asking. "Surely the question should be, why not you? Okay, so you've had a bad morning, who hasn't? But over the years you've demonstrated on more than one occasion that you're more than capable of running this place. Look at all the times you've stepped in to help out when Rebecca has gone sick or something."

"Yeah, but that was only for the odd day here and there and it's been ages since I've done anything like that," Vanessa was quick to point out.

"Maybe, but every time that you were asked, this place was busy, and you always coped with it. Some people might even say you did it standing on your head. And I'd agree with them," he says still meaning every single word as Vanessa's cheeks begin to look a touch rosy as Ritchie continues.

"You're very much a people person, Vanessa. People do like you, not only that, they respect you as well because you don't go screaming and shouting when things go wrong or people make mistakes like I've heard other managers for a fact do. You talk to them. Show them the error of their ways. That's the way I believe a place like this should be run," Ritchie says beginning to truly hope that she'll accept the job.

"It's not that I'm not flattered by this, because I truly am. But I'm not a hundred per cent certain that I'll be the best one for the job," Ritchie was just about to jump in, but Vanessa stopped him in his tracks.

"Please listen, Ritchie, there is a good reason why I'm telling you this… Me and Martin… Well, we've been trying for a family for a little while now and I haven't told many people this, so I'm trusting you to keep this quiet."

"Yeah, of course, Vanessa, promise," Ritchie vowed.

"We've been using IVF Treatment and I'm waiting on results, and if successful, and if it affordable, I'll more than likely be leaving to be a stay at home mum, which is something that we've discussed and agreed on. We think it's better for the baby to have at least one parent at home. So, I don't think it'll be fair to take the job on if I'm only going to be leaving in a couple of months and leaving you in the lurch so to speak.

Ritchie just sits quietly for a minute taking onboard everything that Vanessa has just said to him. "First of all, thanks for being honest with me. I do appreciate that. Of course, I understand you're reasons for not wanting it and I truly wish you all in the luck in the world I really do. But let me offer you a deal. Why not take the job on for now, but only on a temporary basis until I find someone else? That way, even if you do have a baby, there may come a time that you want to decide to come to work, hopefully for us, only then you'll have some management experience under your belt, you could come back possibly straight as a manager. It's worth considering." Ritchie leans back in the chair hoping that he has done enough to persuade Vanessa to at least seriously considering what he's offering, as she had to think to herself Managerial Experience, albeit in a temporary basis, wouldn't look at all bad on the CV if she were ever to come back to work after giving birth.

"Only temporary?" she asks.

"Honestly, only until I can find someone else," he tells her truthfully.

"I'll think about it, Ritchie alright, promise you I will. When do you want to know by?"

"Well for preference, just as soon as you can, but I'm happy to give you until Friday as Rebecca not leaving just yet, give you a chance talk it over with Martin alright. It all seemed to be fair enough as Vanessa agrees before leaving the office and immediately makes a beeline for the changing room and gets not only her coat, but also Caroline's, as she had decided that they could both use a nice lunch hour right about now. Which Caroline had no choice in the matter.

The nearest coffee shop, which was a local and well-kept establishment, was only about four or five doors away from their shop, there were a few customers in there chatting away minding their own business, but not exactly full which was why in no real time at all, Caroline had her Latte along with Ham and Cheese Panini while Vanessa was very happy with her Cappuccino and Chicken Salad Sandwich as Caroline asks, "This is on you right?"

"Yes," Vanessa was happy to inform her.

"Oh good, seeing how you dragged me out," Caroline says smiling.

"Yeah, sorry about that, but had to talk to someone, and not much better than you," Vanessa says.

"Hey, no need to be sorry, I'm getting a free lunch out of it and you know me, always like a natter so, what did Ritchie want you for? Did he make any sexy eyes at you?" Caroline asks with a naughty grin.

"No he did not, and even if he did he wouldn't get anywhere with me, and you're a happily married woman and old enough to be his mother I mean, what are you like?" Vanessa says.

"Yeah, I know, got a lovely husband who I wouldn't cheat on or trade for anything but, I'm still allowed to fantasise, and I've had more than one over Ritchie as my toy boy," Caroline says still with naughty thoughts going through her mind.

"Anyway, you're not going to believe this," began Vanessa. "They only offered me Rebecca's job when she leaves."

"Really! Wow, that's brilliant news, so happy for you Vanessa honestly, well done, you deserve it," says Caroline genuinely happy for her friend.

"Thanks, Caroline," Vanessa says as Caroline then couldn't help but sense there was something not quite right.

"What's wrong? You're going to take it aren't you? You'd be mad not to, think of the extra money to start with."

"To be truthful, I haven't decided yet. Said I'll let him know by Friday at the latest," Vanessa begins by saying as Caroline still looked somewhat astonished by what she was hearing.

"What do you mean, you'll let him know by Friday? You should have bitten his hand off there and then for it. Everyone knows that you're more than capable of doing the job and how many years have you've been here, more than enough years now?" Caroline says as she begins looking more closely at her friend as her intuition was clearly telling her something. "What's wrong, Vanessa?"

"It's Martin," she answers sighing heavily.

"What about him? He's alright isn't he?" asks Caroline.

"Yeah, well, I think he is," Vanessa starts by telling her. "It's just, Look I know that I don't normally do this sort of thing."

"Do what?"

"Answer his mobile. Never even really thought about doing it before. But he was in the shower and I thought to myself that it might be important. Work or something…"

"And was it?" Caroline interrupts by asking.

"It was some woman by the name of Wendy."

"Oh really."

"Yeah, said she was phoning about a part for her Fiesta. I think that's what it was she said, anyway, nah, she made that up on the spot I'm sure of it," Vanessa says mulling over what she heard once again.

"What are you thinking, Vanessa?"

"Not exactly sure, but I just can't help but keep thinking that there's something really not right about this," Vanessa says now looking more directly at her friend.

"Something like what?" Caroline asks as they both continue looking at each other both now mulling over what Wendy had said until Caroline suddenly says. "No, not Martin, he wouldn't," she says, shocked that Vanessa had even contemplated that thought.

"The more that I think about that phone call, and about the fact that she couldn't hang up fast enough once she'd finished speaking, seriously suggests, Caroline, there's something really not right about this. And it's not just this phone call. There's been a few other things over the past few weeks. I got home from your birthday meal and his phone went off, message alert it was, now normally he'd answer straight away, especially if he thought it was anything to do with work, but on this occasion he just ignored it. Didn't think nothing of it at the time as he was being a perfect husband and all romantic.

"Then before, when he went out looking for teabags and a nice Victoria Sponge which we could have whilst sitting down together and watch a film which we had been planning to do all week. He was hours, literally hours, and when I phoned, he didn't answer. Said that when I did not only was he driving at the time, but he heard his phone drop underneath his seat. Could have done I suppose. Also said that before that, took him ages to find that Tesco's Metro, claimed the sat nav was knackered. This isn't that big a place is it? He could have asked directions of someone. Also, he could have phoned the second he stopped the car, he knew that I would be worried about him.

"I hate thinking like this about him because I know that he wants to be a parent just as much as I do, and he works hard. So, hard in fact that the other day he came home with these bruises on his chest where he fell on that concrete floor at the garage. But that if he is seeing someone else? Not sure if I could cope with that at all."

Caroline instantly took hold of Vanessa's hand as the last thing that she wanted to happen was to see was her friend fall apart.

"Now listen to me you. I don't believe for one second that Martin would do anything like that to you. He loves you and he wants a family just like you do."

"You think so, Caroline?" Vanessa just had to ask.

"Yes, I do. Jesus, there aren't many good men around in this world but I honestly believe that Martin is one of them Vanessa." Caroline begins as reassuringly as she could before saying. "If I'm wrong, I'll happy eat a pair of my husband's boxer shorts after he's worn them all day, alright."

She trusted Caroline. Probably just as much as anyone else could trust a person. Knowing this, began to make Vanessa feel somewhat better.

"Yeah, you're right, Caroline. He is a good man and I know that he's desperate to be a father. Maybe it's the waiting to find out if the treatment will actually work this time that's causing me not to think straight at the moment," Vanessa says beginning to breath properly again.

"Yes, maybe it is. Things will happen for you, you've just got to give it a bit more time that's all. And while you're waiting, come here, let me tell you more about my fantasises over Ritchie." Then, giggling like teenage girls, Caroline began to whisper something in Vanessa's ear which soon brought fits of laughter from them both, but Caroline, even though it became difficult to do so, had to keep on whispering, as this was surely not for the rest of the Coffee Shop to hear.

10

Despite the icy wind that would easily cut through the thickest of coats and chill the warmest of hearts. There were still plenty of people willing to brave the elements as Christmas was only two weeks away, the shopping had begun in earnest and the Christmas Spirit was clear.

Even though things seemed to be on the up, Wendy still wasn't quite in the festive spirit just yet. Her injuries had now virtually healed up and she'd had some luck in earning some money as well, which was why she was waiting just on the outskirts of the town centre, in her sensible clothes and looking down the road towards the Tesco Metro which she can just about see knowing that The Sailors Arms and the thought of having a medicinal brandy, just to keep out the cold certainly was a tempting one. But that thought then soon had to quickly disappear as in his recovery lorry, Martin was coming up the road, waving happily through the windscreen the very moment that he sets eyes on her, she waves back, just as happy to see him. Maybe even more so as her heart now was most definitely skipping a beat. He parks up not too far away from her and when he gets out and begins walking towards her he may not be the movie star type of man, in fact virtually nobody would give him a second glance if he walked straight past them, but to Wendy he didn't have to be a movie or even a rock star, he was undoubtedly the most special person in her life right now, or maybe ever has been, but she remained keen not to let that show too much. If at all.

"Hello there, you," he says smiling before giving her a gentle hug which Wendy welcomed.

"Hello there you as well. How are you, you okay?" she asks returning the hug.

"Yeah, all ok, you?" he says.

"Yes, looking and feeling a lot better now thanks," she begins by saying. "And look, got something for you.

"Oh really," his eyes open wide in surprise.

"Yeah, it's right here and please, please, accept it Martin," Wendy says reaching into her coat pocket and produces some money which she plants firmly into Martin's hand before closing his fist and keeping it closed. He knew exactly what this was and why she'd done it, but it still didn't give him any pleasure in taking it.

"Please, Martin, don't get offended now, but there's a little extra, just to say thank you for being there when I really needed someone. I really was going through a rough patch, was having no luck whatsoever, hardly any food in the cupboards, bills were mounting up and I'll be honest with you, I was getting scared, really scared. I've never been in that sort of position before, so I had no clue what to do.

"Until I bumped into you that night. Yeah, I took a beating a couple of weeks ago but apart from that, I've had this feeling going through my veins, that things were going to get better. And very slowly but surely, they have. I can get back on top of my bills again, there's food back in my cupboards and fridge again and I honestly believe it's because I met you again Martin. Like you've been sent to me from the heavens as a lucky charm or something. Please Martin, take this, and the little extra, for me, it would mean a lot to me seeing how I had to ask you in the first place."

"Look, Wendy, you really don't have to pay me back now if you don't want to, especially with Christmas just around the corner. Wait until the New Year if you want, make sure you get some more money behind you in case you have any bad luck again," he says which almost reduces her to tears in appreciation, but she fought those tears back.

"It's fine Martin, honestly I promise you it is. You should know me by now, I always pay my debts."

"Okay, pay what you owe. Like rent, electric, and things like that, get that sorted first before thinking about paying me back. And you've no need to give me any extra, I'm not a Loan Shark or anything like that," he says quite insistently.

"I know that you're not Martin. It's like I said, that's just something to say thanks, that's all. Please take it." Martin remained very reluctant to take any of it. He didn't give her the money just to receive it back, especially with extra on top. He just wanted to help her out as he couldn't bear the thought of her suffering after he'd picked her up from the hospital. And there was no way that he would see her without food. Not a chance in hell of that.

"Are you absolutely certain that you're able to do this?" He just had to ask one more time.

"Yes, Martin, honestly, I can do this. Please take it. Really would mean the world to me if you did," Wendy says refusing to release the tight grip that she still had on his fist.

"Alright, alright, you win, I'll take it okay," Martin

says which makes Wendy happy indeed. "But don't ever forget Wendy, if you ever need anything again, and I mean anything, then you only have to ask me alright, and I'll always do what I can for you."

"Yes Martin, I know all that alright," she says smiling that she had someone like him in her life. Even if it is as only a friend.

"Right," begins Martin, "we're both now agreed that this is now my money."

"Yes, Martin," Wendy wholeheartedly agrees.

"Good, now that we've agreed on that, what are you doing now?" he asks.

"Well, nothing really why?" she asks.

"Well, you see, I've literally just come into a bit of money, so let's go and get something to eat. My treat obviously," Martins says hoping that she'll accept his invitation.

"Yeah, okay then, if you're sure, what about work Martin," she asks.

"Soon sort that out," he says taking out his mobile, opening it up, finds his business partner Rick, and begins texting and mutters loudly. "Just going to do some Christmas Shopping, any breakdown's let me know and I'll deal with them."

"Are you sure about this Martin?"

"Yeah of course, no problem. I done the same for

him yesterday, so it's fine," Martin says as within literally a couple of seconds of sending they both hear 'Ping'. Martin looks at his phone. Sees that there is a reply to his message, he shows it to Wendy who could clearly see it was from Rick. 'Yeah sure, no problem, see you later'. "You see, told you it'll be alright," Martin says happily.

"Okay, fair enough, if Rick says it's okay, then let's go," Wendy was more than happy to agree. And not just because Rick said it was alright, far from it.

"Right, come on, it's bloody freezing just standing around here. I know a decent enough place in town where we can get a decent breakfast," he says as they head off into the town centre.

Maybe they were both seeking for a little bit of extra warmth. Maybe it was the sight of all the Christmas Decorations that were hanging everywhere giving everything and everybody that Christmas Spirit but whatever it was, it prompted Martin to take a gentle hold of Wendy's hand which she in turn offered no resistance as it just felt like it was the most natural thing in the world to do. They continued walking, without a care in the world as if they were back in the days of their relationship which Martin was particularly enjoying, so much that he oblivious to the fact that they had just walked past the Travel

Agents where his wife was working today and were soon to be stood outside a department store window which had a huge display of Santa on his sledge being pulled by his reindeer who's legs moved as to simulate them running through the air.

They both marvelled on how realistic it looked, especially with Santa's huge smile. They moved just as close as they humanly possibly could as Wendy then laid her head on Martin's shoulder to which he responded by placing his head on top of hers and planting a gentle kiss through her soft brown hair onto her forehead which made her tingle all over and take a tighter hold of his hand.

Neither one considered moving for the moment as they looked into each other's eyes using the reflection of the window. Neither one said anything for now, possibly for the fear that if you speak about a wish, it may not come true as again, they both naturally when it was time to move on.

They were soon sat down in a local and well-kept establishment, sat at the centre table surrounded by all the Christmas Shoppers who were busily discussing things like the icy weather and debating whether or not it should have been an XL size jumper instead of just a L for her sister.

The bacon sandwiches which they both had now

in front of them were both made from thickly cut bread and the bacon itself was just a delicate crispy along the edges. Exactly the way they both like it with tomato ketchup readily available for them.

"Tell you what Martin, not that I'm complaining or anything because this looks lovely, but you've got to stop treating me like this, could get used to being spoilt," Wendy says just as she takes her first bite while Martin looks on waiting for some sort of approval from het before trying his. Wendy's eyes lit up the very moment she began chewing was all that he needed to see as he then takes his first bite.

"Wow, this is lovely," Martin begins as Wendy agrees by just nodding as she was enjoying every moment before eventually swallowing.

"You're so right, Martin, lovely thick bread, plenty of tomato ketchup, and the bacon done to perfection to make your mouth water whilst chewing. My compliments to the chef, whoever that may be." Wendy starts by saying before having a mouthful of coffee and speaking again.

"To be totally honest with you Martin, I wasn't entirely sure if you'd meet me today or not."

"Why?"

"Thought that you'd be angry with me after I'd phoned before texting your mobile first the other day.

And I'm guessing that it was your wife that answered. I'm so sorry Martin. I know that I promised that I'd always text first. But I was in a right state. Just been with David…"

"David?"

"Yeah, David, my ex-husband."

"Was that the one who…"

"What, attacked you the other week? Yeah, it was. I honestly didn't know he was there or even that he'd been following me, honestly if I'd known he was doing anything like that I'd sorted it out Martin."

"Wendy, Wendy, it's okay, I know you would have, look at me, I'm okay, nothing serious or broken, just a few bruises that's all," were his reassuring words but that still couldn't stop Wendy from feeling guilty about the whole thing.

"I should have reported him to the police or something."

"No, Wendy, it's fine, all over with now and forgotten okay. Was he giving you hassle again?" he asks.

"Don't know if I'd call it hassle. Let's just say we put things to bed once and for all," she tells him.

"Fair enough then. But I must admit, think it was a good job that Vanessa didn't see my face when she told you that you'd phoned," he says.

"Give you a fright did it?" Wendy asks.

"Yeah, you could say that, that's why from now on my mobile stays exactly where I can see it at all times," Martin says still feeling the sense a relief from that night as Wendy thought about breaking into a giggle but looking at how serious Martin looked right now, she thought better of it.

"Like I said, I'm so sorry Martin, I promise it won't happen again," she assures him.

"Yeah, alright Wendy, I know that you won't, think we've both learnt a little lesson there. And I think she bought what you said about parts for the Fiesta. Is that what you used to drive is it?"

"Yeah, I had a Zetec once. Liked that car, until it was taken away from me thanks to him, I'd like to think that's all in the past now, but being honest Martin, there are days where I just stop thinking about it…" Wendy just continues talking about the life that she had with David, which began to fall on completely deaf ears as, out of the corner of his eye, through the window, he could see Caroline walking in what at first appeared to be a straight line for this coffee shop. Sheer panic set into him, he knew that he would be trapped, nowhere to go, especially as to where they were sitting, because if she were to walk in there would be no way in the world that she couldn't fail to spot him.

It suddenly occurred to him where it was exactly where he was, more to the point, who was working only a few doors down. He had no clue what to do, he wanted his marriage and Wendy to be separate, that way he always thought he could go on seeing Wendy, even if it was just only as friends, and nobody would get hurt, as he had no explanation worked out in advance for just such an emergency like this and she'd had known him long enough to know if he was telling any lies, so if Caroline was to walk in now and see him, then people could get hurt, namely his wife, as Wendy just continued talking about her past with David, not noticing the panic that was still in Martin's eyes as Caroline was getting closer and closer and the only saving grace for Martin right now was the fact that she was too pre-occupied on her mobile to notice anything else for now but she still heading towards the coffee shop, so close in fact, that if she were to reach out right about now, she could easily take hold of and turn the handle, and she'd be in and totally ruin Martin's world.

But suddenly she stops. It looked as though that whoever, it was she was talking to, and had now said something to stop her dead in her tracks. She looked annoyed about something. More annoyed at herself more than anything else, maybe she'd forgotten to do something. But whatever it was, Martin was silently giving thanks to Almighty God that she had now done an about-turn and was now walking away.

"You know something Martin, that's one quality that I've always really liked about you. You're a real good listener... Earth to Martin, come in Martin," Wendy says wondering where he was wearing such a distant expression on his face.

"What?" he asks.

"Are you alright, Martin, you look like you've just seen a ghost or something?" Wendy asks smiling and finishing off her sandwich. "That was lovely, thanks again."

"Great you're finished, glad you enjoyed it, reckon it's best I'd get back to work."

Martin says appearing very keen to suddenly get out of there which Wendy couldn't fail to notice.

"What's all the rush about, Have I bored you with my life story again. Do apologise for that but there are times that when I start, I just find it difficult to stop. But you already know that about me don't you? And anyway, you haven't finished your sandwich yet," Wendy points out to him.

"Erm, I'll take it with me," he says as he immediately wraps it up with the nearest napkin that he can find. "You ready?"

"Yeah, yeah, if you want to go now," Wendy says as she makes sure she finishes her coffee first as Martin, more ushers, then leads her out which she finds his behaviour a little strange especially as they were holding hands like lovers without a care in the world less than an hour ago and now it appeared he didn't want to be seen with her at all.

"Is everything alright Martin? Seriously, tell me, have I done something wrong because if I have, then I'm sorry," she says quite seriously. But Martin for now, was to pre-occupied with looking around the town wondering where Caroline just might have gone to whilst at the same time leading her away as far as possible from the Travel Agents.

"No, it's alright, honestly, but let me give you a lift back home, it's cold, can't have you walking in weather like this," he says still looking around and not at her, which Wendy really appreciated, but his behaviour was still confusing her.

"Yeah, a lift would be great, thanks, appreciate it. But if we're going back to your lorry now, why are we go the long way around?" That was a good question. Which caused Martin to stop and think for a minute. "Well, it's like you said isn't it. There's no real reason for us to see each other now, so I thought I'd take this chance to enjoy your company for as long as possible because who knows when I'll ever get to do it again."

"You always could turn on the charm when you wanted to, couldn't you," she says without being able to resist taking hold of his hand one more time, which was something that he only allowed as Caroline, and most importantly his wife, were now nowhere to be seen.

11

Martin pulled up only a few yards away from McDonald Street flats, there wasn't much in the way of Christmas Spirit visible here as there was barely a decoration in sight in any of the windows, and as the skyline was dark, grey, with clouds looking as though they were just toying with everyone to unleash their lashes of heavy rain when they indeed felt like it. "Now, that's an ominous looking sky if ever I've seen one," Martin says.

"Yeah, it's pretty grim," Wendy agrees as Martin looks at all the windows that he can see.

"You got your decorations up yet then?" he asks.

"No, not yet. I'll do it in the next day or so. Got a nice little tree which has lasted a few years now and all being well it'll last a little while longer. Some tinsel, couple pictures, Santa and things for the window. Should look alright."

"That'll be nice then."

"Yeah, it should be." Neither one could think of anything else to say for an awkward minute or two.

"Well, suppose I'd better be getting back to work," Martin says, which was the last thing that Wendy wanted to hear.

"Yeah, suppose you better don't want Rick thinking that you've totally abandoned him," she says, which were words that Martin didn't want to hear. "Is it okay if I still text you now and again. I promise I will not phone first unless you say so."

"Well yes, of course it is, you can text me anytime you want in fact, I insist that you do okay, especially if you need something, anything, alright." He says as they smile at each other before Wendy places her hand on top of his.

"Thank you for everything, Martin, I truly mean that, and if there is anything that I can do for you, please ask me okay."

"I will," he says then, and even as it was the hardest thing that they've probably had to do since they don't know when, they let go of each other's hands. Martin was hoping for just one more kiss, even if it was just on the cheek, but he was to be disappointed as very reluctantly, Wendy gets out, not even looking at him to begin with, it was only when she went to close the door that she made eye contact with him.

"I don't suppose that you'd…"

"What?" Martin asks.

"That you'd want to come in for a cup of tea. Least I can do for you I suppose, after you, spoiling me yet again." She looks in hope at him which she was unable to hide, but he Martin didn't mind, as he could hide how happy he was to be asked.

"Yeah, that'll be great. But it'll only have to a quick one mind," he says.

"Said the Actress to the Bishop," was Wendy's off-the-cuff answer which had them both giggling as Martin locked up the lorry and Wendy lead the way.

"Welcome to Palace 'Ala' Wendy, not quite Buckingham, but it keeps me warm and dry," she says opening her front door and was only too happy to welcome him as her guest, which Martin was only too happy to be. He closes the door behind him and even though she had made a concerted effort to keep the place clean and tidy, which he could see that she had, nonetheless, he still was far from impressed by her humble dwelling, as he was sure that she was far better than to end up in a tower block whose flats were hardly big enough to swing the proverbial cat in and, as he wasn't claiming to be an expert on the subject, but he was certain that he saw signs of damp on the wall as he walked in. And as for her cheap kitchen table and chairs, well least said, as he knew that he wasn't in any position to judge her, and nor would he. He was only too happy to sit next to her on the sofa taking the first grateful sip of his tea.

"Thanks for this, it certainly hits the right spot," he tells her.

"That's alright, like I said, least I can do for you," she says with a smile.

"So, how long have you been living here then?" Martin asks thinking that no matter how she answered, it was way too long.

"Umm, about three years now, I think. I know it's not exactly The Ritz but, it's home and keeps me warm and dry," she tells as Martin felt certain that he could see another patch of damp by her window.

"Hey, at least you're not homeless eh Wendy," he says trying to be positive for her.

"Yes, there's always that," she answers taking another sip of her tea which was when, and just like when they were walking around the town centre only a couple of short hours ago, it just felt natural that they sit quietly and look into each other's eyes with neither one in any rush to break the silence just yet.

"What are you thinking about," Martin asks.

"Oh, nothing much really, just thinking," she answers.

"Well, like what exactly?" he asks.

"I'm thinking how much I just want you to stay with me right now so I can make up it all up to you for leaving you the way I did all those years ago, and never let you go ever again and you'd would never want to leave me as I'd make you so happy, give you everything that you ever wanted," is what Wendy wanted to say right now and no doubt many more things besides, but she knew that she couldn't just yet. "Oh, just nothing in particular."

"Well, for nothing in particular, you seem to be putting a lot of effort into it," Martin couldn't help but observe as he smiled and wondered what was really going through her mind right now. Was it the same as him? Even though he knew it was so wrong of him to be thinking just how happy he now believes they could be together. Not just for now, but forever. They could both only wonder as for now, neither uttered a single word as they were both fighting the urge to kiss, and it probably wouldn't end there.

"Look Martin, it's been a lovely day, but then again I didn't expect anything less when being with you, but I reckon that it might be for the best if you leave now," she says, but not with any real conviction.

"Why?"

"I think we both know why Martin," she says deliberately avoiding any more eye contact with him.

"So, you felt it too then. Knew that you did, just like when you rescued me a few weeks ago. Thought I might have just imagined it, that's why I never really said anything about it, but obviously I didn't. The spark is still there isn't it."

"Spark?"

"Don't play innocent Wendy. We both know exactly what I'm talking about. That spark. That chemistry which first brought us together, back when we were kids. It hasn't left has it? We both know it," were his words which certainly hit home with Wendy as she knew only too well that he had hit the nail right on the head.

"Look, Martin, I think it's fair to say that we were each other's first true love, so of course there's always going to be feelings there for each other. Wouldn't be natural if there wasn't. But it isn't as simple as it was back then. You're married now. You got a wife and a home to think about. We just can't pick up and start again like nothing happened…"

"So, you would think about getting back with me then if things were different?" Martin leapt in causing Wendy to literally jump back in her seat.

"Well, yeah, of course I would, but things aren't different are they. I won't lie to you Martin. This morning when we were walking around the town centre holding hands, it was like we'd never split up, I didn't have a care in the world and that was also the happiest that I'd ever been since god knows when. So, like I just said, there's always going to be feelings between us, but it isn't right that we act on them, is it Martin?"

"Isn't it?" he asks in what looked like a near desperation.

"No Martin, it isn't right," which she hated saying with a passion just as much as the love that she was now feeling for him.

"But what if we could act on them?" he asks.

"We can't."

"But what if we really could Wendy. And I mean we truly could?" he says with an exact passion as she just had saying her last words as Wendy finally manages to look at him and seeing his passion, just had to say to him.

"Think I know where this is all going now. Please Martin, really think about what you're doing. Are you sure that you want to risk everything that you have now for a chance with me? Your wife, your home and you never said, do you have any children?"

"No. Not yet. We've been trying for years but with no luck. Went on that IVF Programme a while ago but we haven't had any results back yet," he explains.

"Oh Martin, this can't happen, it's not right," she begins to protest. "And what if it comes back positive and you're going to be a father, then what Martin? Are you still going to throw it all away on me? You seriously going to do that?" Her eyes were clearly begging him to think about what he was going to say next. Begging him to serious take minute or two before giving any sort of answer, but it was no good, he already decided what he needed to say.

"Think of it this way, even if the test does come back positive, and it turns out that I'm not going to be entirely happy with Vanessa, I could end up doing more harm than good, and then what? Could easily end up getting divorced and the kid is suddenly part of a broken family, would that be fair on the kid then?"

Wendy had to concede that what he just said did make some sense. In fact, quite a lot of sense as he continues. "Look, if the test does come back positive, I'll do everything that I can to support the baby, I mean, what sort of man do you take me for? But I just know in my heart of hearts, that it's you that I'm meant to be with Wendy. And you know that you're meant to be with me. If I've got that wrong, then tell me to leave, right now, tell me to leave."

"Would you really leave if I told you?" she asks.

"If that's what you really want to happen, then yes," was his answer.

"Then, alright Martin, please leave, before all this gets way out of hand," she says somewhat tearful as Martin didn't move one muscle. "Martin, I just asked you to leave."

"Yeah, I know, but you didn't mean a single word of it, did you? Well, did you?" Martin asks which rendered Wendy momentarily speechless. Because they both knew that he was perfectly correct in his assumption. The very last thing that she wanted was for him to leave, in fact, she just couldn't bear the thought of losing him from her life again.

"I'm not a homewrecker Martin," she says.

"I know you're not Wendy. If anyone is a homewrecker around here, it's me, and me alone, alright. That's going to be my burden to carry alright," he tells her in the hope that it would make her feel better." It didn't exactly make her feel a lot better, but it didn't make her any worse either.

"You have to give her a good Christmas Martin. You must give her a great Christmas you promise me you will? You owe her that much at the very least," she tells him.

"Does that mean what I think it means?" Martin excitedly asks.

"Dunno, what did you think I meant?" Wendy answers.

"Oh, come of it, Wendy, you know full well what I'm talking about," he says remaining excited as Wendy laughs nervously.

"Yeah, I do know what you mean. But honestly Martin, you really want to do this, with me? I'm a prostitute Martin. Hardly, a high-powered career girl that's made it in life and not exactly the type of girl you take home to meet your parents," she begins by saying. "But there's something else that you need to know."

"What's that?"

"I can't have children, Martin. Me and David did try for quite some time until we found out that there's something wrong with my tubes, so you do really need to think this through." Her last comment really hit home with Martin because being a father was something he really wanted to be and has done for quite some time.

"Well, my parents have already met you, haven't they? They liked you back then and I see no reason why, even though they do like Vanessa a lot, they won't like you again now. Just won't tell them about what you've been up to lately, let's face it they've no need to now. And we can move somewhere else if you want. I'll offer my half of the business to Rick, it might be a bit of a struggle for him to begin with, but I'm sure he'll take the chance of being his own boss of his own business. That'll give us some money to start off with. I reckon I can find another job because, without meaning to blow my own trumpet, I'm good mechanic, I know that. We'll be alright Wendy. May be a bit tough at first, but we'll get there, and we'll be happy together, you'll see. As for children well, maybe, just maybe when we're all sorted, think about adoption or fostering perhaps."

Wendy didn't say anything straight away as she knew only too well that what he said about adopting or fostering, he really meant, which she thought was wonderful of him to say, there was no doubt in her mind that she absolutely loved him.

"Look, Martin, this is what we'll do. You have Christmas with Vanessa and whoever you have planned to be with, and after that, if you still feel the same, then okay, we'll talk some more and start making plans, is that fair enough?"

"Yeah, yeah, of course, if that's the way you want it, got no problem with that at all, alright, that's what we'll do but I'm going to tell you now, I'm not going to change my mind Wendy, I promise you that I won't. It's you that I want to be with, I know that now. In fact, I've never been so certain of anything else," Martin says feeling on top of the world as he just couldn't stop himself throwing his arms around Wendy and holding her tight, feeling like he never wanted to let her go which she didn't mind in the least as his eyes started to close as he looked as though he was drifting off into dreamland.

Martin suddenly wakes with a start, alone on the sofa, wondering what had happened, and where Wendy had gone. He looked out the window and the sky had gone dark with the late afternoon winter darkness. He suddenly checks his phone and thankfully for him there were no missed calls or messages at all, which was a relief as he hadn't missed any call outs or more importantly, anything from Vanessa. He rubs the sleep from out of his eyes and stands up, shakes himself off, still not quite believing that he had dropped off to sleep and begins looking around for Wendy. "Wendy," he calls out.

"Oh, hello sleepy head, back in the land of the living, are you?" she asks.

"Yeah, it looks like it," he says, not knowing where her voice was coming from. "Where are you?"

"I'm just in the bedroom, won't be a minute," she answers as he takes it upon himself to go into the kitchen and put the kettle. He didn't think that she'll mind too much.

"Do you want a cup of tea?" he asks.

"Go on then, that'll be lovely," she says sounding incredibly happy as he then switches on the kettle and starts to rummage around the kitchen cupboards for cups. Which he soon finds, milk was next in before finding the teabags.

"Wendy, forgot, do you take sugar?" he calls out.

"No need to shout Martin, I'm only here," she says as Martin laughs and turns around to see her stood in the doorway. His laughter and extremely good mood were soon to vanish as he looks at her stood there casually in her working clothes. She'd opted for denim mini-skirt, tight fitting dark blue jumper which showed off her ample assets to their fullest. It was heels tonight instead of the thigh-high boots, but nothing could beat fishnet stockings and the deep red lipstick shone under the kitchen light which she had now switched on, and she looked even better now she didn't have to put layer upon layer of foundation on to cover the bruising. What are you staring at Martin?"

"Well, you," he answers with his mouth now wide open.

"Me?"

"Yeah."

"What, don't you like the outfit? Was is it, the shoes maybe? Or is it the jumper? Thought I'd better put one on tonight seeing how cold it is out there and yes, I'll be taking my big coat as well. Can't afford to get ill again," she says looking at him for his honest opinion on her look. He just stays speechless. "Is it the skirt then?"

"You're going out tonight, are you? I mean, seriously, you're going out tonight?" he asks.

"Well, yeah, that was the general idea," she tells him wondering why it was it seemed like he had a problem with this.

"Well, you can't go out can you. I mean…" Wendy stops him right there.

"Hang on Martin, what do you mean I can't go out? Since when can't I go out, huh?"

"Well, since earlier, like we decided. You can't have forgotten already surely," he says still in shock at what he was seeing.

"Decided what Martin? Since we both agreed that we'd talk again after you'd spent Christmas with your wife and whoever else it is you're going to be spending it with," she was very clear in pointing out to him as he looked back suddenly remembering that she was perfectly correct in what she had just told him, but he still hated it.

"Please don't go out Wendy. Please. I'll get you some more money just as soon as I possibly can, you won't starve or go without I promise you that," he says with eyes imploring her to listen. She knew that he had her best interests at heart and believed that he would keep to his word and give her anything and everything that he was able to as she walks over and embraces him.

"I know you would, Martin, I do know that, but you got to listen to me now. I don't want to go out, I've never wanted to do anything like this, never, but this is what I've had to do to survive before you came along and will have to keep on doing until, well if we do finally get together…"

"We will be together, I promised you that," he says holding so tightly as not just her potential lover, but also his arms felt so protective of her and Wendy did love the feel of it before she pulls herself away so as to look him in the eyes, which she needed to do before telling him.

"I do love you Martin, okay, I really do, but until we're officially together this is still my life unfortunately. I'll do you a deal, until we're together if that's what you decide, I promise, I absolutely promise you, that I'll be so careful because I know that you're worried about me, but the last thing that I want is to take another hammering or anything, alright," she place a gentle kiss on his lips, when he wanted to return but by placing her finger onto his mouth, she put a stop to it because they both knew that it wouldn't stop at just kissing.

"I'm worried for you," he tells her.

"I know. I'm worried for me as well but if I do get even the slightest hint of trouble tonight I'll contact the police straight away, okay," she assures him.

"Why don't you call me?" he asks looking a touch offended.

"Not tonight Martin, go home to your wife and be with her alright and don't worry about me, I'll be fine. But I wouldn't mind a lift if there's one being offered. Just to the Tesco's just up from The Sailors Arms, can get my cigarettes from there." Martin just looked deflated. He knew that Wendy was going to go out whether he liked it or not and there was nothing that he could about it.

"Yeah okay, course I will. But only because I get to spend a few minutes with you," he says.

"Aww, you are charmer," she says as they both began laughing a little as that was all they could for now to relive the nervousness which they both felt. "Just get my coat," she says before kissing him gently on his nose leaving just a smudge of lipstick there which she quickly wipes off for him.

When they arrived by the Tesco's, it may only have been just after five, but it could have easily have passed for midnight judging by how dark the sky had become and the icy air was still most definitely there as Wendy then came out of the Tesco's with her cigarettes and quickly lights one up. "You know that those things will be the death of you in the end," he tells her.

"We've all got to die of something haven't we," she quickly responds before going on to say. "But until that comes, I shall enjoy these because it's a well-known medical fact these can be one of the best forms of stress relief going."

"Is that a fact?"

"Yes, it is," she tells him grinning before taking an extra-long drag just to prove her point and blowing it all out slowly. "Ahhh! That's better, needed that," she says as the cigarette was clearly giving her a great amount of pleasure.

"Oh hello, fancy seeing you here."

The very last thing that Martin wanted to do was to turn around and see who it was there, because he knew by the sound of her voice exactly who it was. The terror that Wendy could see clearly in his eyes suggested that she now knew who it was. He couldn't avoid her though, especially as now she was only a few feet away from them both.

"Oh, hello there, how are you? You've finished early haven't you," Martin says trying to act as calm and as casual that he possibly could which wasn't easy as inside he was shaking like the previable leaf.

"No, it's gone five now, Martin, I've just found out about this Tesco's and was going to try it to see If I can find something nice for our tea. Oh, I'm sorry, I wasn't interrupting anything was I?" Vanessa asks as Martin wasn't able to think fast enough.

"No, it's alright, your husband, which I'm guessing that he is," Wendy begins as Vanessa nods. "Your husband very kindly helped me as I'd broken down on the main road just before you get into town and after fixing the problem, he'd made sure that I got here just to on the safe side so I wouldn't be late for work tonight," Wendy says as they both secretly prayed Vanessa believed her.

"Oh, that's nice of you, Martin, so what was the problem?" Vanessa then asks.

"What did you say it was again, erm, Martin, is it?" Wendy says.

"Fan belt snapped. Luckily, I had another one with me, so it didn't take too long to fix," Martin says still trying desperately to keep his nerves under control.

"Yes, thank god you did otherwise my boss wouldn't have been too happy with me, I've already been late once this week," Wendy says smiling trying to make everyone at ease.

"Do you work near here do you?" Vanessa asks.

"Yes, behind the bar of The Sailors Arms. Just a bit further down the road and take the first left. Do you know that this is the first bit of trouble that I've had with this one, that's why I usually go with Ford, there normally pretty reliable, and I've always had a thing for the Fiesta Zetec," Wendy says patting affectionately the roof of the Zetec that she was stood next to. Anyway, best get going, boss will kill me otherwise, thanks again Martin, hope you both have a lovely evening." Wendy smiles her best friendly smile, well, the best that she could manage in this situation as then walks briskly away towards The Sailors Arms as Vanessa didn't look at all impressed by her fishnets and heels. Certainly not the look that she'd be seen dead in.

"I've heard about that Sailors Arms," begins Vanessa, "meant to be a bit rough and definitely not the sort of place I'd like to have a drink in."

"Yeah, I've heard the same about it as well. Best to be avoided by all accounts," Martin says as he suddenly remembers to kiss his wife.

"Well, better late than never," she jokingly remarks. So, what do you fancy for tea?" Martin ponders this as he begins to feel a lot more relaxed now that Wendy has gone as Vanessa didn't seem to suspect anything untoward had occurred.

"Tell you what. Why don't we have a little treat. Let's get a Chinese, what do you say?"

"Chicken Chow Mein, Prawn Crackers and Spring Rolls and a nice bottle of something to wash it all down with?" she asks in hopeful anticipation.

"Yeah, why not, it's almost Christmas, let's spoil ourselves," he says as Vanessa eyes lit up at the very thought of this and he couldn't resist showing that the age of chivalry wasn't quite dead yet and opened the door of the lorry for her which she was happy to see, before he gets in and they drive away to enjoy a night in together which, looking from around a nearby and discreet corner, Wendy couldn't help but feel envious of.

12

S uppose it was asking too much for it to snow, but it was still a nice sunny, but cold Christmas morning as Wendy was enjoying her morning coffee whilst sat in her living room looking at the window and her Santa and snowmen pictures which, although may not be the most expensive of decorations, but they managed to bring some of the festive spirit into her flat, just like her small green artificial tree and what tinsel she had left after all these years again, just like the pictures in the window, brought enough *Good Will To All Men* into her flat for her to be satisfied with. Especially as she read, and not for the first time this morning, the text that Martin had just sent her over.

'My darling Wendy. Merry Christmas and I hope you like the flowers that I sent you. I don't know whether it was fate, or just luck that brought us together after all these years apart, but whatever it was, I'm so glad it happened. I know that you're the love of my life, the one that I was truly meant to be with, and it won't be much longer now, I promise you that Wendy. Merry Xmas again, talk soon xxxxxxxxxxxxxxxxxxxxxxxx'

"I hope so Martin, I really do," she says quietly wishing that they were together right now sharing their first Christmas back together as a couple. But for now, she has to be content not only with his text but with the very impressive Christmas bouquet of flowers which she had received from him yesterday which had pride of place on her coffee table as she takes another sip of her coffee, just relaxing for now on her sofa. She planned to have her little bit of dinner quite late in the day just so she could relax in front of the television and watch whatever the first Christmas movie was that came on, it just happened to be one of her favourites *The Snowman*.

*

Even though an extra half an hour or so sleep would have been very welcome, she just couldn't manage it, Vanessa began to stir, yawn, and then stretch as a beaming smile appears across her face realising that it is now Christmas morning, which was one day of the year which she always enjoyed as more often than not, her inner child usually kicked-in.

Her first thought of the day though was to give her husband a nice big, long hug. "Merry Christmas my gorgeous hubby," she says turning over with her arms already to put around him convinced that she would be falling straight into his. But to her surprise, he wasn't lying next to her, nor was he anywhere else to be seen as the bedroom door suddenly opens and the light is switched on.

"Jingle Bells, Jingle Bells, jingle all the way," were the very jolly words then being sung as Martin enters carrying a breakfast tray and what suspiciously looked a Christmas present on it as well. "Ho, ho, ho, Merry Christmas!" he bellows out before giving another couple of lines of jingle bells.

"Merry Christmas to you to. And what's all this, breakfast in bed, again? How wonderful, but you really shouldn't have," she says but obviously delighted that he had made the effort to do so.

"What, of course I should have, it's Christmas Day and you deserved to be spoilt," he happily tells her before planting a kiss on her lips.

"You spoil me enough, especially over the last few days. How many times lately have you brought me breakfast up now?" she asks looking at the full English which was now on her lap and she was unable to refrain from licking her lips.

"You're worth it," he says sitting down next to her as Vanessa just couldn't help but wonder about something?"

"What are you all dressed for?"

"Because I'm picking up your mum and dad in a little while, remember?" As Vanessa suddenly remembers.

"Oh my god, yes, so you are. Good job you remembered as I'd forgotten all about them," she says with a giggle.

"Fancy forgetting about your own parents on Christmas Day," Martin begins. "You're a bad daughter you are. You almost don't deserve this," he says as he hands her a slender looking box which had been especially gift wrapped in gold paper with white satin ribbon and bow.

"Is this really for me?" she asks.

"Of course it is, Merry Christmas," he says as Vanessa just holds and holds onto it wondering what on earth it could be. "Aren't going to open it then?" he asks. The answer was yes as Vanessa couldn't wait any longer as then, in a flash, she ripped of the ribbon and paper to reveal a white leather box who's edges were trimmed with gold stitching. Vanessa then, had her breath taken away when she looked inside as it was the 18-carat gold bracelet which she had seen in the jeweller's window just last week.

"Oh, my God, Martin! How did you know?"

"It wasn't all that difficult, seeing how you were literally drooling over it the very second that you clapped eyes on it," he knowingly said. Vanessa loved it even more now than when she first set eyes on it, but a sudden rush of guilt then swept through her.

"Oh, Martin, you really shouldn't have done this. It was way too expensive and don't try and say that it isn't because I saw the price of it. Please say that you kept the receipt just in case you may have to take it back and exchange it for something a bit cheaper as honestly I wouldn't mind at all," she says sincerely but Martin was having none of that.

"You bloody what! Take it back. Like hell I will. This is the present that you wanted, so it's all yours okay, no argument about it. And it doesn't matter how much it cost, because you're worth every single penny," he says giving her a kiss on the cheek before not being able to resist helping himself to some of her baked beans.

"Well, if you're really and I mean really sure that you can afford it Martin," she says.

"Yes, I can alright, so stop fretting about it."

"Okay, if you insist."

"Yes, I do insist," he says before she then closes the lid.

"Won't put it on just yet, got to start preparing the dinner in a little while, don't want anything happening to it," she wisely says before taking hold of his hand and placing it tenderly onto her stomach. "Who knows Martin, maybe this time next year we'll be helping a little boy or girl open their first Christmas presents." Her face now said it all. This is what she desperately wanted now more than anything in the world, and she wasn't going to hide that fact from anyone.

"Well, you just never know Vanessa eh. You just never know," was all Martin could say to her right now as he knew only too well that it would be wrong of him to even think about building up her hopes too much as usually they would say to each other, "you're going to be a super mum," to which the reply would normally be something like, "you're going to be a great dad," but nothing like that was said to which normally Vanessa might just ask if there was anything wrong, but, this being Christmas Day, and her parents are coming, and once again he had waited upon her 'Hand and Foot', she let this one go before she reaches under the bed and produces a neatly wrapped present for him. "Merry Christmas darling," she says.

"Oh, thank you very much," he says before excitedly opening it to see a bottle of expensive CK

Klein Cologne which he appeared incredibly happy with.

"You sure it's okay. I know it isn't as expensive as what you paid for mine. But I remember you saying that you liked it," she says.

"Don't be daft, it doesn't matter how much it costs. It's great you know that I like this stuff and I know that you do as well." He opens the bottle and puts and little dab around his neck and leans over Vanessa so she could smell it.

"You're right, I do like it as well," she begins by saying. "Right, when you get to my parents' house, do me a favour will you."

"What's that?"

"Keep them there for as long as you can please. That'll give me a chance not only to enjoy this lovely breakfast that you've done for me, but also get myself sorted out before getting on with the dinner alright."

"Keep them there? How?" he asks.

"Well I don't know, think of something. Insist on having a cup of tea or something, chances are mum won't be ready when you get there, you know what she's like for fussing about what she's wearing. Talk to dad about City, you know how you both like to talk about that. Just something to give me a chance to get going here okay."

"Alright then boss, whatever you say. So, I'll be as long as I can be alright. And thanks for the present. It's lovely. "Martin then kisses Vanessa on the forehead before leaving her to enjoy her breakfast.

It went down a real treat. Every mouthful was savoured and enjoyed. Just like the long shower that followed before getting dressed and heading downstairs. Before she actually began the Christmas dinner, Vanessa wanted to enjoy the peace and solitude, just for a short while so, after making herself a cup of tea, she drifts into the living room just to feel the Christmas Spirit that has been created in there. With the white artificial tree which nearly touches the ceiling decorated in thick red and gold tinsel along with a multitude of lights, baubles and not forgetting a star on top and with some other shiny wrapped presents underneath it. She then switches on the window display and 'Merry Christmas Everyone' to now shining brightly for all the world to see. The row upon row of Christmas cards lined up along the mantlepiece but the ones saying, 'Happy Christmas to my dear wife' and 'Merry Xmas to a great husband' took pride of place next to each other. What tinsel that wouldn't fit on the tree was placed around the edge of the mirror that hung on the main wall and there was no way that she would decorate her living room for Christmas without some mistletoe hanging down from the lampshade. She liked the way that it all looked. All set for a family Christmas at home. "Right, can't stand around here all day, dinner will never get cooked at this rate," she says before dashing off to the kitchen.

"Right, that's the veg boiling nicely away. Roasties in the oven along with turkey and pigs in blankets. Christmas Pudding and Mince Pies all set to go, the table laid, so it's time for a little medicinal wine, I think. Just to keep me going and help to get into the festive spirit," she says pouring herself a small glass of white wine which just so happened to be right next to her and already conveniently opened.

"Mm, nice drop that, must remember that label for the future," she says just as the front door opens and her husband walks in very closely followed by her incredibly happy to be their parents.

"Hello!" Martin calls out.

"In the kitchen!" Vanessa calls out in reply as literally it took just a few more seconds for her face to light up on seeing the three people that she loved most in the world walk into the kitchen. "Hello, and Merry Christmas to you both," she then says.

"Merry Christmas to you my darling," says Jill.

"Happy Christmas," says Alan as Martin just takes

a step back so that Vanessa could have a moment with her parents. Which she dearly loved having.

"Oh, I'll tell you what, that food almost smells good enough to eat," Alan says with a chuckle.

"You, cheeky git," Vanessa replied not being to chuckle along with her dad.

"That's right you, don't be so horrible to her," Jill says gently slapping him across the head.

"She knows that I'm only teasing, don't you my girl," Alan then says still chuckling away.

"Yeah, and it's a good job for you that I do," Vanessa says.

"Martin."

"Yes Jill."

"Why don't you take Alan out from under our feet so we can get on with the dinner," was Jill's suggestion which neither one of them minded in the least.

"No, mum, I didn't invite you around here to do any cooking. You're here to relax and have a good time okay," Vanessa strongly told her mum who had no intention of listening to her.

"Don't be so silly, you should have known that I wouldn't let you do all this by yourself."

"But, mum…"

"Don't but mum me alright," Jill begins before

turning her attention to the two lads. "Right you two, out, don't care where you go just as long as it's not too far because I don't think this will take too long," Jill very clearly told them.

"Right, seems that we're not wanted here, Martin," Alan says as, just taking a chance, opens the fridge and just happens to find two cans of lager which he shows to Martin.

"Seems you're right there Alan. Tell you what, just for a laugh, I've still got the table football set up in the shed if you're up for that?" Martin asks.

"You just lead the way Martin," Alan says as they both run out like two little boys who have finally been let out after being in trouble.

"Look at them," Jill says. "Mention football and beer and they're just little boys aren't they because I'll never understand what it is about football that gets them all worked up."

"Neither will I, but if it keeps them happy…"

"And out of our way," Jill jumps in to say.

"Didn't say that though," Vanessa was quick to point out.

"No, but you were definitely thinking it weren't you eh? Come on, tell the truth, you were weren't you" Jill says knowing her daughter only too well as she couldn't find an answer. "Knew that you were.

So, how's everything?"

"Yeah, can't complain at all. It's been good," Vanessa says but Jill was in no way convinced that she was telling the truth.

"Are you sure Vanessa? What about what you told me about the other week?" This made Vanessa stop and think before speaking again.

"I have to be honest mum, got no complaints at all. He's been great, especially over the last few days. Just can't do enough for me. It was breakfast in bed again this morning and look what he bought me for Christmas." She opens the box and Jill couldn't fail to be impressed.

"Wow. Now that wasn't cheap at all was it?"

"No, mum, it certainly wasn't, he most certainly put in the overtime to get me it for Christmas."

"Yes, I can see that," Jill says still momentarily not being able to take her eyes of it.

"So, it's like I said mum, I can't complain as he's always been good to me, and still is."

"Well, must admit, he's never given me any cause to be concerned for you in anyway. So, what was all that about the other week then you were telling me about?" Jill had to ask.

"I don't really know mum. Honestly couldn't tell you. Maybe this was one time that my gut feeling just got it wrong," Vanessa says with a shrug of her shoulders.

"Oh, alright then, can't always be right I suppose. But you know if I ever find out that he's done anything like that, they'd be sliced off in an instant. And your dad my come across as all smiles and just wanting a laugh, but you don't want to see him lose his temper, and I mean really lose it I can promise you that." Jill was quick to tell her daughter, who just smiled back.

"I know Mum, thanks."

"Good. Anyway, changing the subject slightly now, have you heard back from the doctors yet?"

"No, not yet. But I'm hopeful that this time it will be our turn to be lucky. So, don't you go throwing away your knitting needles and patterns just yet alright," Vanessa tells her as Jill promises that she wouldn't as they were all still in her beside cabinet as they continued getting the dinner ready.

The lads were soon to be called in from the shed with the match delicately poised at two each and they would have to play the second half at a later date as for now, it was time for the Christmas Dinner, the time of year that Vanessa especially had been waiting for. And she was so happy that her immediate family were all together as Martin, being head of this household carved the turkey and served before they all sat down, toasted each other, and began enjoying the dinner. Vanessa was enjoying herself more and more with each passing minute seeing everyone laugh and smile and really get into the Christmas Spirit as Martin, was so attentive to all of their needs. Whether it was making sure that they all had enough to eat and drink, nothing was too much trouble for him. Even when Alan and Jill left after spending a simply wonderful day with them, Martin insisted that he would clean up the kitchen, which wouldn't be Martin if didn't.

And when he was finished, he went into the living room to find it empty. "Vanessa!" he called out but got no answer, which brought him to the conclusion, that she may have already gone to bed. So, after locking everything up and turning the lights out, he ventured up the stairs to the bedroom and his thoughts were right, as there she was, now changed into her nice soft towelling dressing gown and had fallen asleep on the bed. Must have been that last wine she had, well, he did warn her about it. But there was no way that he could be angry with her as she not only looked so peaceful, but also she looked so happy as he switches of the lights, makes sure that she has enough of the duvet, before getting into bed himself, knowing that he had given her the exact Christmas that she would have wanted.

13

Good morning x and Happy Boxing Day x
Oh hello and Happy Boxing Day to you xx

How was your day yesterday? xx

It was okay quiet just me and the telly x yours? Xx

Yeah it was okay. Had her mum and dad for the day they seemed to enjoy it xx

That's good then xx

Yeah xx What are you up to today? Xx

Not much probably just another day in front of the telly x Elf is on sometime today always makes me laugh that does xx What about you x

Going to spend the day with my parents today x She's in the shop buying them a few things so I thought I'd text you know may not get a chance later xx

Thanks for thinking of me x

No problem x Know where I'd rather be though x

Down the pub with all your mates watching the football no doubt lol x

Ha-ha no lol xx

Strip Club then lol xx

Only if you were working lol xx

Spend all your money on me would you lol xx

Every single penny x and you know it xx

Ha-ha you always were a charmer xx

Hahaha I know and you love it x

Yeah, I do a bit lol xx

You got enough to eat now x

Yeah, I've got enough in now for the next couple of days thanx I'm getting back on my feet now but I'll never forget what you did for me xx

It's okay you don't have to keep on thanking me x always going to look out for you aren't I? x you know that x

Yeah you have told me that more than once lately xx

Because it's true xx

Yeah I know xx

I've really thought about what we talked about the other week xx

Talked about? Xx

You know what I mean xx

Yes I do xx

My mind's made up x I know what I want and what I have to do now xx

I'm begging you Martin please be certain about this xx

I've never been so certain about anything xx

Really? Think about what you're giving up x A home a marriage and you could be becoming a father anytime soon and that's sometime that you could never have with me remember I told you that I couldn't have kids xx

I haven't forgotten that xx

I just don't want you to feel let's say 6 months or so regret doing this xx

The only thing that I'm ever going to regret is not taking this chance to be with you xx

Ok then x you know that I'm going to be here for you xx

Are you really? Xx

Yes Martin I am x When I saw you a few weeks ago by The Sailors and that Tanya was all over you couldn't believe that I was seeing you again after all these years and I also knew that I had to make up for leaving you x I now know that I shouldn't have done that x my life would have been so much better if I'd stuck with you from the beginning xx maybe this was a second chance or something xx

Yeah maybe it was xx don't get many second chances in life xx

No we don't do we xx

That's why I want to grab this one with u xx

If u r sure xx

Positive xx

Then I'm here xx

You don't know how happy you've just made me knowing that you feel the same xx can you give me a few days sort things out? Xx

Yeah of course take all the time that you need and do what you have to do ok xx

Ok xx thanks xx best go now she's coming out of the shops x be in touch soon I promise xx

I know that you will xx be here waiting for you xx

14

It was that fine and misty rain, the type which guarantees that you get wet, no matter how well you might be covered up. Not usually the sort of weather that people actually relish going out in but seeing how this is New Year's Eve, they'll be plenty who will no doubt brave it.

Even though she really didn't want to, Wendy did go out the previous night, still got bills to pay plus, she hadn't heard anything from Martin since that text conversation on Boxing Day and even though she understood perfectly that he did have things to sort out, it still would have been nice to hear from him. Even if it was just one text saying, 'good morning xx' or 'how are u xx'.

Whilst sat at the kitchen table, now not really wanting the cheese sandwich that she had done for herself as the nerves were beginning to kick in along with her mind starting to work overtime going back to the Boxing Day conversation. Was he really going to do what he said he was and give up being a natural father, just to be with her? Would it be fair of her to expect him to do such a thing no matter how much she loved him? Or very simply, was he just okay? All these things and many more thoughts were almost spiralling out of control whilst going through her mind, what she needed now was to hear from him as she continually stares at her mobile, praying for a call or just a text. Couldn't even finish one cigarette before lighting up another one.

*

"Should old acquaintance be forgot tra a la, la la, la," sang Vanessa as she literally skipped and danced her way into her living room as above the mirror on the main wall hung a banner which read 'Happy New Year Everyone' before taking hold of polish and duster and proceeded to clean anything and everything that was humanly possible to clean and no sooner than that was done, out came the hoover and god helped anyone who got in her way now as nowhere on the ground floor was safe from the suctioning power of her almost new hoover as she never looked happier doing what a lot of people would consider mundane chores as the singing merrily continued.

*

"Right, that's all the cheesy nibbles got, crisps, sausage rolls, cocktail sausages, pasties and quiches. Yeah, got all of them. She'll be doing all the sandwiches later, so don't have to worry about that. Sweet stuff? Chocolate Cake, yup, Strawberry Cake, yup, and boxes of chocolates got those. Just the important things now," he says looking towards the wines, beers and spirits aisle. "Right, did she say that we needed red wine or not? Better check, especially with Jill coming around because I know that she lies a drop or two of it. Oh, and Gin," he says reaching for his mobile from his jacket pocket but all of a sudden, he sees a frail old lady, at roughly halfway down the drinks aisle clearly struggling so much to reach up to the top shelf that she might just have an accident herself at any moment as everybody was just walking past not even bothering to ask if she needed any help. This would not do Martin decides as he walks straight up to her. "Hello there, my love, can I help you?"

"Oh, thank goodness for that, yes, could you please help me. I'm trying to reach that bottle of Bailey's up there, would you mind passing it down to me?" she asks so sweetly.

"Of course, I don't mind," Martin says as he

happily reaches up and passes down the bottle which she had pointed out and puts it into her basket.

"Thank you so much my dear. I always like to have a little drop just to see in the New Year as my Bert won't touch it. He always prefers a drop of his whisky," she tells him.

"That's alright my love, you're very welcome. Anything else I can get you while I'm here," he asks.

"No, no thank you, you've been very kind," taking his hand in gratitude. "Happy New Year to you," she says, and he wishes her the same back before she shuffles of towards the checkout.

"Be honest, I can't be wrong if I do get a couple of bottles of red and a bottle of gin. It'll get drunk sooner or later," he says to himself before getting all that was necessary before he himself proceeding to the checkout, but not before he made a cursory look through the trolley, checking that he now had everything he thought was needed for tonight's little get together as he made his way down to the checkout and took his place at the back of a very long queue where it seemed plenty of other people had the same idea as him.

"Well thank god that's over and done with," Martin says as it gave him great pleasure of getting rid of the shopping trolley, placing it back with all the others before getting into the car and as speedily as possible, made began his journey home.

Seeing his home coming into view was a very welcome sight and thoughts of a nice hot fresh cup of tea began to fill his mind rather than being stood in a queue with people becoming agitated over having to wait for so long and quibbling over the price of this or the price of that with whoever was working the checkout. As he then pulls up onto the driveway he couldn't fail to notice that the front door was wide open and there were three large black bin bags which were tied up and looked quite full sitting on the doorstep. "Thought it was unlucky to through rubbish out at New Year," he says to himself, not really making a big deal out of it though. He parks up, and begins taking all the shopping out of the car and into the house. It took him four trips to do it all and leave it all at the bottom of the stairs before making one final check that the car was all locked up before heading back indoors and at the very moment that he crossed the threshold from out of absolutely nowhere Vanessa came screeching out towards him.

"Where the hell do you think that you're going!"

Martin stopped dead in his tracks, she was in a such a foul temper that he'd never seen her in before.

"What's wrong? What's happening?" he asks

totally shocked by what he was seeing.

"You bastard!" He'd never even heard her swear before, he was dumbstruck. "After all the years that I've given you just for you to treat me like this!" as then she slaps him so hard across his face that she's leaves a handprint for all the world to see.

"OWW! Vanessa, what's wrong with you? What's this all about?" he asks totally in shock.

"You don't know!" she shouts.

"No," he answers.

"Well maybe this will give you a clue," she says forcing him to take hold of his mobile which he suddenly realised he'd forgotten before he left home this morning. "Why don't you check your messages? Go on, do it! Do it now!" she demanded that he do. It was a clear hesitation that he done what she wanted as it was slowly becoming clear what just might have happened and sure enough, there was a new message from Wendy. "Anything there you think I should be told about? Well! What's the matter? Got nothing to say? Open up that late text you got. Go on, do it. It's for you isn't it? So why don't you read it? If you don't open it up and read it I bloody will and read it out for all the street to hear!" She meant it, this was no empty threat, he knew it, so all he could now was exactly what she wanted him to do and open it up.

'Hiya, Martin, just thought I'd txt as I've not heard from you for a few days x Hope that u r ok. Have you told her yet? We r still going to be together aren't we? Xxx'

He couldn't bring himself to look at his wife. Couldn't think of one single word to say in his defence, that was probably because he knew he had no defence.

"Yeah, I bet that you've got nothing to say because I've gone through all these messages from her. 'Oh I love you Wendy'. 'I love you to Martin'. 'The only thing that I'm going to regret is not taking this chance to be with you'. Really, is that what you want is it, the chance to be with her, is it? WELL IS IT! They don't let me bloody stop you!" she screams as not too surprisingly, one or two of the neighbours curtains, began to twitch as Vanessa then goes over to the three large black bin bags, picks them up, and literally hurls them at him with tears of anger by now, streaming down her face.

"There, you can pick up the rest of your stuff when I tell you to alright. I knew there was something going on. I just knew it. And I think I know as well. It's that one from the other week isn't it. That barmaid, or so she claimed from that Sailors Arms place. The one who said had broken down, broken fan belt or something wasn't it. You know the one. The one who was dressed like a right tart. Barmaid! That's a laugh! Probably some sort of prostitute would be more like it." The look in Martin's eye was now one of wondering how the hell she could have guessed.

"Oh, so I'm right then, it is her, don't deny it as that look in your eye tells me I'm right. I should have seen it earlier because when I thought back to that day, there's you saying that you've literally just worked on her car because you said that you followed her just to make sure that nothing went wrong again, but your hands were clean, spotless even. You didn't even smell of oil, grease, or anything like that when I kissed you, but for some reason I must have just blocked it out. Maybe it was because I believed that there was no way that you'd do anything like that to me. Or that there was no way that I thought anyway that you'd want to go with any woman who dresses like that.

"But obviously I was wrong. Well if it's cheap and seedy and dirty is what you want then as far as I'm concerned, that's what you're going to have from now on, alright. Now go! Go on get out now because I've told my mum and dad everything and they're both on their way around here now. So, get out of here now! Go!" she says pushing him as far as she was capable of doing.

Martin genuinely looked devastated. Even though he hadn't lied to Wendy about wanting to be with her, Vanessa deserved to be treated a lot better than this and he knew it.

"I'm sorry, Vanessa, I really and truly am," he softly says but she wasn't at all interested in listening to him as she forced him to take his Christmas present to her. "And you know what you can do with that don't you? Also, don't give me that you're sorry. You're only sorry that you got caught out!" she says and with just as much brute force as the first time, she slapped him across the other side of his face, again leaving a handprint for everyone to see before she storms off back indoors leaving the front door wide open in the process, but there was no way now that Martin would even think about going in after her. All that was left for him to do now was exactly as she said, just go. Which is what he did as he gets back into the car and begins to drive off.

No sooner is he off the driveway and heading away from the house, from the other direction, Jill sees him and the temptation to follow, stop him, and find out how exactly he's hurt Vanessa, then hurt him, was indeed great, but her first thought had to be of her daughter as she parks on the driveway, and like a Bat out of Hell, races into the house calling

"Vanessa!" As she does so her instinct directs her to the living room and they were proved to be correct as Vanessa was on the sofa, totally broken-hearted, sobbing profusely and needing her mother as she sits down and throws her arms around Vanessa as if she would never leave her side.

"It's over, Mum. He's gone. That's it now, I don't ever want to see him again," Vanessa says.

"Oh, my darling, are you sure it's definitely all over? With absolutely no going back?" Jill asks.

"No. No, Mum, there isn't. It's all over for good. There's no way that I'd have him back now," and despite the tears of sadness, this was very clear. "He was going to leave me Mum."

"Yes, so you said on the phone. Are you absolutely sure about this Vanessa?" Jill had to ask.

"Yes, Mum, I saw all the messages."

"Messages to who?" Jill asks.

"All I know is her name is Wendy and that's about it, apart from the fact that I was sure that I caught them together a couple of weeks ago," which shocked Jill.

"No! Where?"

"Not too far from that Sailors Arms pub. You've heard of it, haven't you? That rough place just off the edge of the town centre."

"Yes, I've heard of it. What the hell was he doing around there? Rough as rats around there. Full of drug dealers and prostitutes, so I've heard," says Jill.

"Yeah, I've heard that as well. Don't ask me what he was doing down there but's where I caught them because I was in that Tesco's trying to find something for our tea that night. Claimed that she'd had broken down and he had fixed her car, and he followed her down there just to make sure that the car was all working," Vanessa says still sobbing.

"I just can't believe what I'm hearing," Jill says still holding her daughter just as tightly as she possibly could.

"All true, Mum. Every word. My god you should have seen the state of her. Fishnets, high-heels, mini-skirt the full works. Claimed she worked at that pub but it wouldn't surprise me if she was walking the streets with the rest of the tarts down there. If that's the sort of look that he wanted to see, why didn't he just ask me, I'd had done it for him."

"What, degrade yourself like that?" Jill was surprised to hear.

"Mum, I would have dressed up like R2 bloody D2 if he wanted to. He was my husband. I would have done anything for him. I loved him. I just don't understand Mum, really I don't."

"Oh, I don't understand either my darling. Men are a totally different breed to the rest of us human beings. Think mostly with their privates instead of actually using the brains that they were given. I don't understand it, truly I don't. Really thought that you two were happy together and had a real chance of making it last forever. All you needed was a baby and I'm convinced everything would have been fine and this would have never had happened."

Vanessa lifts her head up from her mother's shoulder and looks straight into her eyes, and without having to say another word.

"No!"

"Yeah."

"When did you find out?" Jill asks.

"Went to the doctors yesterday and he confirmed it. I was going to tell everyone here tonight at the party."

"Oh my god, and he still does…"

"He doesn't know Mum. I wanted to see the surprise on his face as well. Would have made my year that would have. But now I'll never see it because as far as I'm concerned he's never going to know after what he's done to me. He doesn't deserve it. It'll be father unknown on the Birth Certificate." And even though she remained almost inconsolable right now by what had happened, this was something that nobody was ever going to change her mind about.

"Now, Vanessa, I know that he's hurt you so badly right now and you should be bloody angry at him, but he has a right to know about this," Jill says trying to be the voice of reason.

"No, Mum. He's given up any sort of rights as far as I'm concerned now. He's gone and I'm keeping this baby. I'll be alright. I'll see my area manager Ritchie. He'll make sure that I'll be alright."

"Was that the one who offered you that Branch Manager's job not so long ago?"

"Yeah that's right. I'll see if that one is still going and if it is and see if he'll offer it to me again. If not, I'll tell him that'll be interested in the very next promotion that comes along. I'll be alright. I mean it Mum, I will. All I'm asking from you now is stay here tonight. Dad as well if he wants to. Please Mum. If I can just get through tonight then I'll get through it all," Vanessa says and her mother didn't hesitate to answer yes and promise that her dad would be here and not just tonight, but for forever as she refused to let her daughter go.

*

It looked as though she was settled in for the afternoon. The fresh tea and biscuits were on the coffee table, television was switched on, and Wendy was laid out on her sofa watching some made for television Christmas movie. But she wasn't paying too much attention to it, her mind was clearly wandering elsewhere as every few seconds she would checked her mobile for any sort of message that might have arrived or even hoping upon hopes that it would ring. For now, though nothing, nothing at all as all she could do was sit and hope that she would hear from Martin very soon.

The film really couldn't keep her focus on the television screen, so it was down with the mobile and up with the remote control and she began flicking through the channels in the hope of finding something that might just take her mind of Martin. Not an easy task. But it was just the same old stuff that they put on every Christmas and New Year time which hardly gave Wendy much satisfying viewing and Martin was still very much on her mind as then there was an unexpected knock at her front door which made her instantly sit up and wonder who an earth it could be as she stood up and began making her way towards her front door.

The very second that she was in the hallway and looking towards her front door and the frosted glass panel, she came to a grinding halt. Because she could definitely see that it was a man stood outside but was it the man who she longed for it to be? No, it couldn't be, could it? There was no time to lose as she just had to find out and raced to the door and opened it to realise that her prayers had been answered and it was Martin stood there.

He obviously looked like he had his tail put firmly between his legs, carrying the three large black bags that Vanessa had hurled at him and he was still was bearing her mark across his cheek, but Wendy didn't care how he was looking right now as to her, he was not only perfect, but he was here. "Hello Wendy."

"Martin, hi, so nice to see you, but the dustbins are on the ground floor and around the back," she says jokingly and poking each bag in turn.

"I'm here, Wendy," he says.

"Yes, I can see that you're Martin," Wendy says wishing he was here for keeps but until he actually said, she was protecting herself from hurt.

"No, no Wendy, I'm here for good, that's if you still want me." Wendy's jaw fell completely open, which she was powerless to stop after her prayers had now been answered and before he had a chance to say anything else, she grabs hold of him and drags him indoors and slammed the door behind him. "Are you serious?" she asks.

"Never more so," he tells her truthfully.

"What! I mean, how, no what I mean is, what happened? Did you sit her down and tell her everything?" she asks.

"No, she found out." Wendy was gobsmacked when she heard this.

"How?"

"Well, I was out getting some food and drinks as we were planning to have a small get together tonight for New Year. Because I thought I'd give her that as well as Christmas, and I was going to sit her down and talk to her within the next day or so. But I'd forgotten my phone, it was left next to the microwave. So, when you texted earlier, she heard it go off and decided to answer it, and once she did, she found the rest of the messages between us. Especially the ones that we sent to each other on Boxing Day. So, that was it. Understandably, she went mad, threw me out, and now here I am. Maybe not exactly the way I planned it, but if you'll still have me, I'm all yours."

Even though there was some deeply rooted sympathy, as well as some guilt, for the way that Vanessa had found out, this was still probably one of the happiest moments of her life which momentarily she done her utmost to contain. "Oh Martin, I'm sorry. I knew deep down that I should have waited a bit longer and let you sort things out in your own time. Like you said you would. I just got worried because I hadn't heard from you for a while. Really sorry Martin."

"Forget about it, Wendy. Suppose it was never going to be easy telling her about this. No matter when I did it. But at least now it's done with and we can start our life together," he says with nothing but true love for her which had Wendy bursting, almost too tears, with happiness.

"I'm just an old prostitute who can't give you kids Martin. I can't believe that you're giving everything up to be with me."

"Let's get this right here and now shall we. I'm giving everything up to be with the love of my life," he says as without further ado, and not being able to contain himself any longer, he puts his hands ever so gently onto her cheeks and kiss her, re-igniting the love that they shared all those years ago only this time, they were both convinced that the flames would never die out.

Which, for now, certainly seemed to be the case. As two years and one week later, and after moving to a new town, they now have a new home. Martin did sell his half of the business to his partner Rick and even though there were some difficult weeks, he managed to set up his own small garage and eventually get another breakdown business up and running and with Wendy's help. Wendy had now landed a job in a local hospital kitchen, but with her previous management experience, it wasn't too long before she was made up to supervisor. So, it appeared that they had, for now, made the right decision, and were living in happiness together.

15

A further week on from that, it had been quite some time since she had felt nerves quite like she now felt. In fact, not since her interview for the Branch Manager's position that had become available very soon after Martin's departure, had Vanessa felt the butterflies like this. But a phone call to probably the most special person in her life would make her feel at ease about now.

"Oh hello, is that Angelica, is that mummy's special little girl, is it? Oh, gone has she, hello there, Mum."

"Aww bless her, well she always likes to be in on the conversation doesn't she?"

"Yes, I'm okay. I think. It's been a long time since I 've done anything like this."

"Yes Mum, I know that you're right, as usual. I'm divorced now, got to get out there and start living again. And it's only lunch I suppose and as the old advert says, what's the worst that can happen?"

"Alright Mum, I'll phone as soon as I'm back in the office okay. And I'll be around to pick Angelica up after work okay. Give her a big hug and kiss from me, see you soon."

That certainly calmed her down by quite a considerably way, knowing that her daughter was fine and in good hands. She certainly feels a lot better as she leaves her office and goes out into the main shop where Caroline couldn't help but give a playful wolf-whistle the very second that she saw her. "Looking good there, boss. If I was a man, I'd be chasing you alright."

"Don't be daft, and less of the boss alright, you know I don't like that," she tells her for the umpteenth time.

"You deserve it boss, you're earned everything that you have now," Caroline reminded her for the umpteenth time before giving her the final once over.

"Will I do?" Vanessa asks.

"Of course, you'll do. He'd be daft not to want you. Where is it you're going again?"

"Only to that new Pasta Bar a few streets away."

"Meant to be nice there."

"Yeah, I've heard good things about it," says Vanessa.

"Right then, you go and enjoy yourself alright, and don't forget I want all the gory details when you get back okay," Caroline says looking and feeling very proud of her friend that she has managed to bounce back from having her heart well and truly broken.

"There'll be no gory details, it's just lunch. But I'll give you all the goss when I get back alright," Vanessa says as she gives her a quick hug before leaving the shop.

Just over two years ago, hardly anyone would have noticed Vanessa as she started walking through the town centre as (or so she thought at the time) she was just a happily married woman. But what the world could see was a Vanessa who not only had her heart totally broken but also have her whole world come crashing down around her, but now could walk with her head totally held up high. As she was a totally new woman with a renewed confidence who could not only get the job done at work but could raise the child that she so dearly wanted. It was hardly surprising that she turned more than one man's admiring head as she continued on her way.

It was agreed with the man who she was having lunch with, that he would do the gentlemanly thing and be at the Pasta Bar first, so as not to have the lady sit around and wait by herself. From the very moment that she enters her eyes were everywhere looking for him. Luckily, he'd spotted her and had now stood up, waving, hoping to attract her attention, which he soon did and she goes over to join him at the table.

"Hello there, nice to finally meet you in person," she says with a polite handshake and kiss on his cheek.

"Nice to see you as well, really glad you made it," he says returning the kiss on the cheek. "Hope you don't mind, but I've got you a sparkling water because I remembered that you said that this was your lunch hour, if that's okay?"

"Yes, yes of course that's okay, thank you," she says impressed with his thoughtfulness as the waitress then takes the food order as they finally settle in with Vanessa feeling quite pleased with herself that she'd swiped right.

"So, then Vanessa, why don't you tell me some more about yourself?" the man politely asks and already looked genuinely interested to hear her answer.

"Well, not a lot to tell really. Erm, Travel Agent as per my profile. Branch Manager, not too far away from here actually, just on the other side of town. Single mother, just the one, daughter, Angelica, who's just over one year old now," she tells him.

"Oh right, okay, so if you don't mind me asking, why did you get divorced?"

"No, that's fine. He cheated on me," Vanessa told him in an instant.

"Oh, I'm sorry to hear that. And for what's it worth, he's obviously a fool for doing it," he says to which Vanessa couldn't help but feel flattered by that.

"That's very nice of you to say," she then begins by saying. "Why don't you tell me something more about you then David?" You're divorced yourself aren't you?"

"Yes, that's right, but I always make a point of telling the truth about that," he begins as Vanessa was more than happy to hear someone being honest, as well as being very intrigued.

"My marriage failed due to my own selfishness. I was an addict you see. Oh, not drink or drugs or anything like that. No, my addiction was gambling. I'd bet on just about everything, you name it, I'd bet on it. Ended up losing everything but like I said, at the time I was just being selfish, she begged me to get help, but I wouldn't listen until it was too late that was. But, I did get the help that I needed, beat the addiction and now I like to think that I've really learnt my lesson, and now, I can move on with my life.

ABOUT THE AUTHOR

Paul 'Pops' Westlake, the 'Pops' coming from the days when serving in the Royal Navy. Born in Plymouth, where he still lives today and is the second of four children and has had a variety of jobs down the years such as working on Building Sites, Road Sweeper, Bookmakers Cashier, Hospital Porter and currently employed as a Security Guard. This book, *'By Pure Chance'* is the third that he has written the first two being *'The Flatterys of Nodnol Hall'* a comedy crime thriller and the romantic comedy *'The Ghanaian Woman'*.

Printed in Great Britain
by Amazon

56399181R00142